# EYE FOR AN EYE

# EYE FOR AN EYE

## THE UNBELIEVABLE MR. BROWNSTONE BOOK THREE

### MICHAEL ANDERLE

DISRUPTIVE IMAGINATION

EYE FOR AN EYE (this book) is a work of fiction.

All of the characters, organizations, and events portrayed in this novel are either products of the author's imagination or are used fictitiously. Sometimes both.

Copyright © 2018 Michael Anderle
Cover by Andrew Dobell, www.creativeedgestudios.co.uk
Cover copyright © LMBPN Publishing

LMBPN Publishing supports the right to free expression and the value of copyright. The purpose of copyright is to encourage writers and artists to produce the creative works that enrich our culture.

The distribution of this book without permission is a theft of the author's intellectual property. If you would like permission to use material from the book (other than for review purposes), please contact support@lmbpn.com. Thank you for your support of the author's rights.

LMBPN Publishing
PMB 196, 2540 South Maryland Pkwy
Las Vegas, NV 89109

First US edition, May 2018
Version 1.02, May 2018

The Oriceran Universe (and what happens within / characters / situations / worlds) are Copyright (c) 2017-18 by Martha Carr and LMBPN Publishing.

# EYE FOR AN EYE TEAM

## Special Thanks
to Mike Ross
for BBQ Consulting
Jessie Rae's BBQ - Las Vegas, NV

## Thanks to our Beta Reader
Natalie Roberts

## Thanks to the JIT Readers

James Caplan
John Ashmore
Sarah Weir
Kelly O'Donnell
Joshua Ahles
Larry Omans
Paul Westman
Peter Manis
Micky Cocker

*If I've missed anyone, please let me know!*

## Editor
Lynne Stiegler

*To Family, Friends and
Those Who Love
to Read.
May We All Enjoy Grace
to Live the Life We Are
Called.*

# 1

A man never disrespected another man in his home. A church was God's house, so James wouldn't disrespect the Big Man by losing his temper and cursing—despite the little punk who had just run into him for the fourth time.

"Watch it, kid," James growled.

The little punk stuck out his tongue and ran from the sanctuary toward the hallway. It led to a small room where some of the kids from the orphanage were helping sort donations.

"This is a church," James called after him, shaking a fist. "Show some fuc— Show some respect."

A quiet chuckle came from behind him, and the bounty hunter turned, a frown on his face. He didn't have time to deal with idiots who didn't like his attitude toward little ankle-biters.

Father McCartney stood there with a box of books in

his arms. He lowered it to a pew and turned to Brownstone.

James sighed, not willing to chew out his confessor.

"He's just a child," the priest reminded him. "Please be mindful of that."

"I know, but still..." James grunted. "I just don't like kids."

"You helped Alison, and she's a child."

James shook his head. "She's a teenager. They can be irritating, too, but at least they're almost adults. They can be reasoned with. Kids are just...annoying. Like puppies, but not as cute. And puppies are easier to train."

"We were all children once, and I don't just mean in the spiritual sense." A faint smile appeared on Father McCartney's face. "Reasoning with children, hmm? I remember when you first came to the attention of the orphanage. We couldn't even communicate with you."

James grimaced. Low blow, talking about his childhood.

"That was a long time ago," he mumbled.

"True enough. Best we could tell, you were probably around three when they found you with nothing but the clothes on your back and a small box. Just some trinkets...and, well, that necklace."

James stared at a statue of Jesus. "I don't remember anything from then."

"I remember it clearly. You weren't the first abandoned child we'd dealt with, of course, but even then I knew you were special." The priest laughed. "You jabbered away in some strange language. It wasn't like anything I'd ever heard." For a moment his dignified manner slipped, and his working-class Jersey accent grew stronger. "We sent samples to forty different translators, but no one had a clue. They said it didn't even *sound* like anything they knew. A few professors at one of the colleges said it had some basic similarities to Xhosa in some of the clicking sounds, but not in the structure or anything else."

James shrugged. He didn't see why the priest suddenly wanted to take a trip down memory lane.

Part of keeping his life simple meant looking forward and not back, especially to a period he couldn't even remember. That hole in his early life bothered him even more because of his otherwise solid memory.

For the most part, he had a photographic memory.

Father McCartney frowned. "We even wondered if you were speaking in tongues, but after consulting with the bishop we all agreed that was not what we were dealing with."

James stared at the priest for a moment. "Did you guys ever think I was possessed?" He'd always wondered, but hadn't dared voice the question before.

"Never for a second. Demonic possession involves *evil* behavior, not *strange* behavior."

The bounty hunter still wondered if his necklace had been touched by a demon. It would explain a lot.

"Okay, okay." James shrugged. "I get it. I was a little weird-looking freak who didn't speak normally. What's your point? Why are we talking about it now?"

Father McCartney sat down in the pew next to the box of books and shook his head. "I've been thinking about it a lot lately. It's still a mystery, James. We don't know what happened to your parents, but a few years later—once the truth about Oriceran came out—we were convinced that you were from there. It made such perfect sense, but then...all the tests, blood and otherwise, confirmed you weren't."

"Earth has produced plenty of freaks even without Oriceran magic. Big deal."

James gritted his teeth. The more they discussed his past, the more he would be forced to confront memories he'd tried to avoid. The fate of his parents remained shrouded, but that didn't mean other bits of darkness didn't lie in wait in his soul.

Father McCartney looked at the statue of Jesus and then at James again. "I think he would have been proud of you."

James burst out laughing, but quickly stopped himself.

*Respect God's house.* "I think Jesus might have issues with my methods. He was a real turn-the-other-cheek kind of guy. I'm a little more Old-Testament."

The priest chuckled. "That might be true, but I wasn't talking about Jesus."

The bounty hunter's stomach knotted as the past bore down on him. He had a good idea who Father McCartney was talking about, but had hoped to steer the conversation in a different direction.

"Who then?" James sighed.

"Father Thomas, of course."

James turned away from the man. "He died young, protecting me. I think both Jesus and he would regret that, considering what a wretched sinner I've become."

Memories flooded in. Father Thomas throwing him a ball, reading to him, giving a stern lecture to some kids who had mocked his odd face. *I grew up around a bunch of* men I called "Father," but I had only one father I can remember—and he died too young.

Father McCartney stood and placed a hand on the bounty hunter's shoulder. "Mankind is fallen. We're *all* sinners." He nodded toward the statue. "His sacrifice wouldn't have been necessary otherwise. I knew Father Thomas well, and I know he wouldn't regret anything that had to do with you."

James' phone screeched, as did the priest's.

"What the hel— What's that?" The bounty hunter pulled the phone out of his pocket.

**LOS ANGELES COUNTY EMERGENCY ALERT SYSTEM: EXTREME THUNDERSTORM ALERT. NOAA TRACKING INDICATES HEAVY STORM ACTIVITY UNTIL MONDAY WITH STORMFALL EXPECTED BY LATE EVENING. ALL RESIDENTS ARE ADVISED TO MINIMIZE NONESSENTIAL TRAVEL.**

James grunted. "A storm? Well, at least the rain will help with all those fires we've been having." He slipped his phone back into his pocket. "I should get going. There are a few things I need to check on."

Father McCartney picked up the box of books and nodded. "Thanks for helping today, and thank you for all the money you've provided to assist the church and the orphanage."

"Just doing my part."

The priest shook his head. "We both know you're doing the parts of ten."

Dark storm clouds gathered on the horizon like some evil Atlantean forces planning an invasion.

James didn't care. He barreled along the highway in his Ford F-350, more than confident in his vehicle and his ability to handle a little rain. He chuckled as he thought about how everyone insisted that self-driving cars would be the future when he was growing up, but presently the roads still mostly belonged to human—or at least humanoid—drivers.

Was it keeping it simple or making it more complicated to let some gadget drive itself?

Maybe in the end, despite all the fancy technology and blather about the future, at some level society knew that James' philosophy of keeping it simple was the best plan for long-term stability. Or maybe once people had realized that magic was real, trying to build paradise using technology suddenly seemed like unnecessarily hard work.

He grunted. Talk about wanting to do things the easy way: the Harriken had imprisoned and tortured Alison's mother because they wanted to acquire her wish, which would be the ultimate in cutting corners. All their power and money and they still craved more.

The bounty hunter's phone rang, snapping him out of his critique of modern society. He pressed a button on his steering wheel to accept the call in speaker mode.

"Yeah?"

"Brownstone," came a familiar woman's voice.

At least, he was almost certain it was her. The call quality was somewhere between crap and shit.

"Shay?" James asked.

"Yeah, it's me." Her voice went in and out, but he understood what she was saying.

"I can barely hear you. You sound like you're calling from a wind tunnel on Mars."

"Look, I'm on a job and in the field away from anything you might call civilization, and I'm not talking about Sacramento. Quality isn't always that great, even with my new fancy satellite phone. Anyway, stop worrying about my shitty phone and more about yourself."

James chuckled. "What do I have to worry about? No one's tried anything stupid around me in...uh," he tried to remember, "days."

"I was checking some of my back messages before I headed toward my main site, and I found something you should be aware of. There's a big hit out on you. Looks like half a million, maybe even a million."

"Why would that be in your messages?"

"I keep an ear to the ground so I don't end up dead."

"Well, fucking great," he rumbled. "Should have expected that. Okay, so someone wants me dead. That's not new, and I've made a lot of new friends lately by killing so many people. Hell, you in trouble, too? Don't tell me they have a higher price on you."

James didn't want to be a target, but the price on his head proved how deeply local criminals had grown to fear him.

Shay laughed. "No hit on me, Brownstone. Just you. *I* don't go out of my way to inform my victims about how I'm the oncoming storm of doom or some shit."

"Good for you, but having a certain reputation makes my life easier. It's why I do it."

"Having a half-million-plus bounty on you is making your life easier?" Shay asked.

He backpedaled just a bit. "Well, it makes my life easier most of the time."

At least that was the theory. He'd worked hard to grow his reputation. Some feared him as the Granite Ghost, others as regular old James Brownstone. Terror was supposed to keep the criminals in check, but this time it'd backfired to the tune of a half million. Or maybe a million.

Shay snorted. "Yeah, yeah. I know this is all some male-ego shit, but whatever. Anyway, arm up, dumbass. This information was fresh, and it sounds like whatever's gonna happen, it's gonna be soon."

"You're sure about this?" James asked.

"Yep."

"Thanks, Shay."

"Assuming you don't die, I'll talk to you later." The field archaeologist hung up.

James heaved a great sigh and shook his head. Part of not getting killed in a dangerous profession was taking warnings seriously.

The bounty hunter had a bounty on him, huh? He should have seen that coming.

James changed lanes. Now he couldn't go straight home. He'd need to stop by his warehouse to pick up a few things in case someone dangerous decided they wanted a quick half-million.

The truth was, until he verified who was after him, he couldn't solve the problem by killing them. Being a bounty hunter hadn't exactly made him a lot of friends in the local underworld—or in North America.

If he didn't hate flying so much, he might have managed to offend thugs on every continent.

Despite all that, James wasn't worried. Shay was out of the country, and Alison was safe in a government-approved magic school filled with witches, wizards, and strange creatures. This wasn't like with Leeroy. The only person he needed to worry about was himself.

"Bring it, fuckers," James muttered under his breath. "I'm feeling pissy, and I'm bored."

---

About an hour later, the bounty hunter rolled into his driveway. He'd picked up his amulet from the warehouse, but he hadn't bonded with it yet. The little trick he'd discovered using a piece of metal affixed to the back had worked out well the last few times, so he'd repeated it. Now he would have quick access to the amulet if he needed it.

James took stock of his current loadout, using both a visual inspection and a quick pat-down. His new gray coat did an even better job of concealing his holsters and tactical webbing than the dusters he'd favored before. Not only that, he was certain he looked less threatening in the gray coat—which could help him avoid unnecessary attention until the last moment.

The bounty hunter smirked, remembering Shay's bitching when she'd seen a picture of it.

*That looks just like that shit you wore in Mexico, Brownstone. Just because it doesn't have holes doesn't mean it's not shit and ugly as hell. Have some damn pride, man!*

Fuck fashion.

James verified the presence of multiple pistols, magazines, knives for stabbing, knives for throwing, potions, his amulet necklace, and even a few jammers in case drones showed up. James was geared up to clear out a Harriken warehouse, kill a necromancer, or humble a top-hat-wearing ferret or two.

A go-case sat in the back seat of his truck, containing even more weapons and fun treats for dishing out death and destruction.

He hoped he wouldn't end up explaining it all to the LAPD. After his recent near-showdown with an LAPD Anti-Enhanced-Threat team, he'd become more aware than ever that some of the local authorities viewed him as more of a threat than an ally.

That worry could wait until later. Right now, the LAPD had to get in line behind the criminals.

The bounty hunter grunted, satisfied. Unless the entirety of the Los Angeles underworld showed up he'd have the advantage, even without using the amulet.

Assuming no one tried to kill him in the next couple of hours, he could even get in an episode of the newly-premiered *Barbecue Wars: All-Stars*.

The buzz around the show had been somewhat overshadowed by the win of Nadina, an elf, in the recently-concluded season of *Barbecue Wars: The Next Generation*, but James could appreciate a show focused on good old-fashioned human pitmasters.

He thought of the man behind Jessie Rae's. *I don't know, Mike. It's still gonna take me a while to get used to Oriceran-style barbecue.*

James hopped out of his truck and hurried to his front door, slamming it once he was inside.

He walked to his basement door. He might not always be able or want to swing by the warehouse in the coming days, especially if he were being followed, so it wouldn't hurt to double-check his weapons and ammunition supplies in the basement.

James unlocked the reinforced steel door's physical locks before placing his hand on the palm scanner. The electronic locks clicked open, but more importantly, his traps were now disabled. Any fool could batter open a door if they worked on it long enough, and he wanted it to hurt if they succeeded.

The bounty hunter pulled open the heavy door and made his way down the stairs. After the errand, it was barbeque show time.

---

A few minutes later, a black van with tinted windows screeched to a halt in front of Brownstone's house.

"You ready, Cartwright?" the driver asked.

The mercenary sitting in the back heaved his rocket launcher to his shoulder. "I've always wanted to use this thing. One of the best high-explosive yields you can get in a weapon of this size."

"Just do it already. We need to move before Brownstone figures out we're here and wastes our asses."

"No one respects quality tools anymore." Cartwright threw open the van's doors and aimed the rocket launcher. "See you in hell, Brownstone, you cocky sonofabitch."

The rocket sped on its way, flame trailing behind, and slammed into the front door, exploding in an orange-red ball of death. A cloud of flame, wood, and metal fragments rained on the street, part of the roof collapsed, and a side wall groaned, cracking and collapsing a few seconds later.

"Damn, that was nice!" Cartwright crowed to his partner.

The mercenary reloaded the launcher and fired at the burning house a second time.

The second rocket blew half the house apart, and the explosion that followed knocked the mercenary back inside the van. The vehicle almost tipped it onto its side but slammed back down, rattling the two men inside.

"What the fuck was that?" the driver asked.

Cartwright sat up, closed the door, and wiped some grime off his face. "Gas lines, I'm guessing. Let's roll. No way the motherfucker survived that."

## 2

The whole house shook. Part of the basement ceiling collapsed on top of a box filled with .45 magazines. The second and third explosions buried more of the basement and provided James an angled view of the inferno above him through the newly-created hole in the ceiling.

The entire house seemed to be on fire—at least what remained of it—although no smoke detectors shrieked.

Yeah, probably no one had ever thought about making them blast-proof.

James shook his head. His ears were still ringing from the roar and force of the explosions, and he was unsure of what the hell had just happened. An earthquake wouldn't have been over so quickly.

The first explosion had sounded familiar, like something he'd heard more than a few times in his life. That kind of sound generally started with a weapon or three.

James pushed through some debris toward the stairs.

Flames eagerly danced at the top, and they and the smoke denied him a more detailed view of whatever remained of his house.

James realized he didn't have much time. He had more than a few grenades and explosives in the basement. If he waited, the fire would make its way down and blow him into a million tiny pieces. He doubted even the amulet could save him.

He yanked his phone out of his pocket and tapped at his security app. He hadn't been so hot on cameras, but with all the crap he'd gone through lately, he'd decided it wouldn't hurt to install a few outside.

CAMERA FEED INTERRUPTED.

James grunted and backed up the feed. The arrival of a black van and the appearance of a rocket-launcher-wielding man in urban camouflage confirmed his suspicions.

What was with the outfit? Was the asshole trying to blend in with the van?

He shook his head. If he'd been upstairs, he wouldn't have survived the first explosion.

"Fuckers," James muttered. "Stupid-ass motherfuckers. You blew up my fucking house. My fucking barbecue grill. *My fucking signed recipe books.*" He let out a long, loud bellow of rage.

Some people never learned. The Harriken had murdered his dog, so he'd delivered the pain a hundred-fold back to them.

Now some asshole had blown up his house. As a minimum they needed *their* houses blown up, and they also needed to be ground into pieces so fine that even a DNA analysis couldn't identify them.

Sirens sang in the distance, and James narrowed his eyes. He didn't want to have to spend a lot of time dealing with questions. He returned his attention to his security app and initiated a remote backup of the last few minutes, then erased the footage.

The police didn't need to get involved—especially given the sheer volume of violence James was about to unleash in LA.

He glanced down at his chest. The fight with King Pyro had demonstrated that when he wore the amulet he'd have at least some protection from fire, but putting it on to flee a burning house didn't seem worth the risk.

The sirens grew closer, and a loud horn honked right outside.

The damned whispers from the amulet had grown stronger with each use, so he wasn't sure how much longer he could use it.

A lot of questions remained about the nature of the amulet, and today's conversation with Father McCartney had only reinforced in the bounty hunter's mind that his ultimate weapon could very well be evil.

That might explain what happened to his parents.

James coughed. Smoke filled the basement now, and the flames had crawled partway down the stairs. The police might have some questions if the rest of his place went up like a roman candle, but that could wait. Pissy AET aside, the cops had already looked the other way several times for him— and this time *he* was the damned victim.

It just so happened this victim believed in dispensing

personal justice. Very bloody personal justice. Or very crispy, in this case.

"Fuck it," he muttered. He wasn't going to sit still and force some firefighter to risk his life when he could get out without help.

He didn't need the amulet. He'd won against King Pyro the first time without it. Escaping a burning house would be far easier.

James bounded up the stairs, arms in front of his face, and charged through the flaming opening where his basement door used to stand. Pain spiked through his arms as fire licked his arms.

The blasted and half-melted remains of the steel door lay a few feet away.

The bounty hunter rushed straight toward the front door, or at least where it used to be. The front of his house didn't exist anymore, which made escaping the raging fire far less of a chore.

James gritting his teeth as he sprinted through the flames.

Two fire trucks were parked on the street, their crews hustling to get their hoses set up.

A firefighter dashed toward him. "Sir, are you all right?"

The bounty hunter waved him off, ignoring the light burns on his arms. "I'm fine."

"Do you have any idea of what happened?"

"Gas leak," James offered nonchalantly. He headed straight toward his truck.

His hands curled into fists. The bastards hadn't blown up his F-350, but it hadn't escaped unscathed. Wood and metal debris were embedded in the hood and the passenger window, including a charred two-by-four. It looked like some giant shotgun had blasted his truck.

If those fuckers had killed his truck, he would rip apart every motherfucking criminal in this city.

The firefighter hurried after him. "Sir, you need to get checked out by a paramedic. And that vehicle doesn't look very safe."

"This truck has saved my life more times than I can count." James hopped inside. When he turned the key and the engine roared to life, but the CHECK ENGINE light was on. Relief warred with the homicidal rage burning inside him.

He patted the dashboard. *Don't worry. I'll get you somewhere for repairs soon.*

The bounty hunter turned back toward the firefighter. "My house just blew up, and it's not exactly morning. The first thing I need to do is find a place to sleep tonight, and *you* need to back the fuck up because I have a shitload of explosive flammables in my basement and there's a good chance they'll go up in a big boom. So move your fucking ass, and get your guys back before someone else gets hurt."

The firefighter's eyes widened and he yelled. "We've got a good chance of secondary explosions. Everyone back the hell up."

The firefighters scurried back as James pulled out between the fire trucks.

James was halfway down the street when he spotted the huge fireball in his rearview mirror.

The singed man had driven for a good fifteen minutes when he pulled into a Costco parking lot to make a call. For a second he wondered if the store sold any Oriceran spices in bulk, but before long his angry thoughts returned to his housing mishap.

The fuckers had blown up his house with a rocket launcher. On some level he could respect the sheer balls of someone willing to do that, but that also meant they weren't practicing anything remotely in the realm of what people would call restraint.

It was like they were him—and no one liked facing themselves.

James grunted. If he stayed in a hotel innocent people might get caught in the crossfire, if not blown up.

"Those fuckers." The bounty hunter slammed his fist on his dashboard. He'd been told someone might come after him, but not that they'd blow up his house. A few bullet holes here and there would have been fine, but the entire building was gone.

He sighed. *Guess I should have had a few backup houses. Lot of fucking good that does me now.*

James yanked his phone out of his pocket. He knew a lot of people who might be willing to help him with a little temporary lodging, but the overlapping part of the Venn diagram that included those same people and people who could protect themselves from rocket-launcher-wielding assholes was damned tiny. There was only one real choice.

"Hello, lad," the Professor answered after two rings.

"Some asshole just blew up my house."

The Professor sighed. "That's rather annoying. How? Magically?"

"Nah. He kept it old-school. Used a rocket launcher."

"That would do it. And you want me to find out who did it?"

James grunted. "Not so worried about that right now. The issue is, I need somewhere to stay."

"I'm not a real-estate agent, lad. Couldn't one of your fine churchmen put you up?"

"I'd prefer the church not get blown up by a rocket launcher. I'm pretty sure there's a commandment about that."

The other man laughed. "I can see how that wouldn't be appealing. So you'd rather my house be blown up? I'm hurt, lad."

"Nah. I figure you're smarter than me so you have a few spare places scattered around in case some necromancer or ancient Chinese general shows up looking for shit you might have. I'm thinking you're a man who deals with powerful artifacts without trouble, so you know how to hide stuff from prying eyes."

Silence reigned for a few beats. "All right. I understand, and aye, I do have a place you could use. A small apartment. There's no paper trail linking me to it, and it's protected against a variety of types of spying, magical or technological. But you'll owe for me this, Brownstone."

"Fine by me. Just try and not send me anywhere that's too fucking far away when you cash in that favor."

"Stop by the Leanan Sídhe in a few hours, and I'll have some keys and an address for you."

"Thanks."

Shay grumbled as she sat on the edge of the soft hotel bed. There was nothing like traveling halfway around the world only to find your target site was now a huge crater. At least she hadn't been in the place when it'd become a hole.

The locals didn't have much useful information to offer, other than something about a group of men heading toward the site and then seeing a massive explosion. The authorities mumbled something about a crashed plane, but the level of destruction Shay had witnessed could only be produced by a military-grade bomb or some sort of magical artifact.

Now that the field archaeologist was back in civilization she needed to catch up on her mail and messages, so she pulled out her phone and started skimming the subject lines of her messages. One in particular caught her eye, and she opened it to read the detail.

"Oh, shit," Shay muttered. "Damn. Guess that explains it." She immediately dialed Brownstone.

The bounty hunter picked up after a single ring. "Hey, Shay. What's up?"

"Harriken, Brownstone."

"Huh?"

"The hit on you. It's Harriken-funded."

James muttered something under his breath. "Not a huge surprise. I figured it was Harriken or maybe Grayson, even though technically the mercs weren't our fault. Not saying I had any problems with what Nicole did."

"Sorry to break it to you, but from what I just read Grayson's looking for you as well. They get a premium if one of their guys takes you out."

He grunted. "I'm glad I'm bringing people together."

"So, anything happen so far? Anyone take a shot?"

James chuckled. "Nothing big. They just blew up my house."

Shay blinked several times, not sure if she'd heard him right. "*What?*"

"Some assholes showed up in a van, and they blew my house up with a rocket launcher. My truck's fine, thank God. But my house is a fucking crater. The initial blasts were bad enough, and then the fire got down to the basement. I'm bumming a place from the Professor. Fuckers. Lost all my barbecue equipment."

Shay wished she were in LA so she could see the expression on his face. She couldn't tell if he was taking the situation seriously or not.

She finally decided to go with "no." "*You* okay, Brownstone?"

"Don't worry about me. If the fucking Harriken didn't get the message before, they're gonna get the message now—even if I have to kill everyone last one of those bastards in California." James sighed. "But I need you to promise me something."

"Sure. What?"

"If something happens to me, make sure Alison's okay. She's all set up financially with the trusts and shit. She just needs someone to have her back and visit her."

"No, Brownstone. Screw that. You're not dying, and you're not doing anything without backup."

James grunted. "I'm not gonna sit around on this, Shay. These fuckers blew up my motherfucking house. I need to make my position clear on what happens to people who blow up my residence."

"I get that. Just relax for five seconds. I'll hop a supersonic flight back, and we can do this together. I don't like how you're giving me speeches about taking care of Alison. This isn't like you. It means your head isn't screwed on right. Wait for me, okay?"

James hung up.

Shay gritted her teeth and slammed her phone down on the nightstand so hard her fingers hurt. She shook them out and looked at her phone, which now sported a jagged crack across the screen.

"This might have been a cheap burner phone, Brownstone, but I'm still gonna make you pay for it," Shay ranted. "All this stupid machismo crap from men and their stubborn asses. Plus… You know what, Brownstone? I'm gonna make you pay for the airline ticket too."

# 3

Jiro Ikeda, leader of the Harriken in the United States, sat behind a rather spartan wooden desk in his temporary headquarters in Los Angeles. He didn't want to breathe the air of a city that stank so much of failure, but the Brownstone situation needed to be resolved and Grandfather required a personal touch.

The Harriken leader stared at the bandaged stump where his left hand used to be. His superior had already shown him great mercy by taking only a hand and not his life, but Jiro knew that any more failure wouldn't be tolerated.

There was a light knock at the door, and Jiro looked up.

"Yes?" he called in Japanese.

A beautiful young Japanese woman in a black skirt, camisole, and jacket opened the door. "Your appointment is here, Mr. Ikeda."

"Send him in."

She nodded and closed the door.

A few moments later, a brown-haired man in an ill-fitting suit stepped inside.

Jiro kept his face blank, even though the man in front of him reeked of arrogance and incompetence. He begged to be humbled.

Mercenary scum. He had no honor. All he did was what he was told.

The Harriken might be considered criminals by many, but they were their own masters—not puppets to be pushed around, like the Grayson mercenaries.

Jiro gestured to a leather chair in front of his desk. "Sit," he directed in English.

The other man took a seat, and an appreciative look appeared on his face. "Nice chair."

"Let's be efficient at this meeting. I have other matters to attend to today."

The man grinned. "You like to get down to business? So do I. I'm here to talk about the money for rubbing out Brownstone."

"Mr. Cartwright, was it?" Jiro leaned back in his chair. "That was what you said over the phone."

"*Sergeant* Cartwright, and I don't like the fact that your people made me give up my gun out there. That's disrespectful to me and to the Grayson PMC Services company."

Jiro gave a faint shrug. "We treat armed men who aren't part of our organization as a threat." His eyes narrowed. "And be aware, *Mr.* Cartwright, that right now you are a guest of the Harriken. *You* will show respect to *me*."

"Listen, pal, I don't give a shit about your jumped-up Yakuza bull—"

Jiro pulled a sword out from underneath the desk and had the tip at Cartwright's throat in a flash. "One cannot demand respect. One earns respect through actions and demonstrations of one's willingness to pursue such actions."

Cartwright slowly raised his hands. "Hey, hey, calm down, Mr. Ikeda. We're all on the same side here."

The Harriken resisted snorting and lowered his sword. These mercenaries played at being soldiers, but without the honor that came with an organization like his own, they deserved no respect. He dirtied himself by relying on such scum, but with the local forces depleted the Harriken needed any help they could find.

Cartwright rubbed his neck and grinned. "Hey, just think of it this way. Thanks to this disrespectful and normally armed man your Brownstone problem is gone, so you need to pony up the cash."

Jiro kept his hand on the sword and rested his arm on the desk. "Pay you? Why would I do that, when you clearly haven't met the terms of our bounty?"

"You can't fuck with Grayson, you know." Cartwright stood and leaned over the desk in a feeble attempt at intimidation. "I want my fucking money."

The sword went to the other man's neck again. Cartwright winced and sat down again. He was clearly unused to not being able to intimidate others.

"If you do that again," Jiro stated flatly, "you die. Do you understand?"

Cartwright nodded quickly and swallowed.

Jiro resisted the urge to skewer the man anyway. However, making additional enemies wouldn't help the

Harriken at this juncture. Still, he would remember this Cartwright's arrogance for the future.

"Look, Mr. Ikeda, I'm just saying I killed Brownstone. I did what you asked. Everyone says the Harriken always keep their word, good or bad. A lot of our guys got killed because you gave us crap intel, so we deserve our payday for taking down Brownstone."

"I believe our rules in this matter were very clear," Jiro replied, his voice flat. "No body, no bounty. And I don't see a body. Do you plan to deliver a body to us? That's fine, or even a head. I'm sorry, we can't accept a hand or limb." He held up his stump. "As you can see, a man can survive losing a hand without too much trouble."

The mercenary stared at Jiro's arm for a moment, an unspoken question in his eyes. "I confirmed entry. I have video of him going in. His house is a fucking burned-out cinder now."

"But you have no video of his body, or even his head. That leaves the possibility that he is still alive, and we'd be fools to pay you for killing a man who might still be alive, don't you think?"

"The body would be extra-crispy anyway. What good would it have done to give it to you?"

Jiro snorted. "Between magic and science, we could easily verify if it was Brownstone's body." He narrowed his eyes. "If you want the money, deliver us the body…or the head as a minimum. Otherwise, don't waste our time. We're not offering to pay for Brownstone's house to be destroyed. We're paying for his *death*."

Cartwright shook his head, his face red. "What if I get confirmation that he's dead from the LAPD?"

The Harriken laughed. "You'll beg the police to confirm this death? Don't you think they'll link you to the crime then, fool?"

The other man gritted his teeth. "I'm just saying they'll report it sooner or later. Murders are a matter of public record."

"Not good enough."

"What the fuck? Him being dead isn't good enough?"

Jiro shook his head. "No. His dishonor of the Harriken was too great. We require his body—or at least the head—so it too can be dishonored."

A look of disgust passed over Cartwright's face. "Okay, I'll see what I can do." He shoved his chair back and stomped to the door.

Jiro watched him leave, his lips pursed. Once Grayson had served its purpose, he'd stab Sergeant Cartwright through the heart.

---

Colonel Grayson sat at the end of the long table that dominated the briefing room. His surviving trusted subordinates were all sitting around it.

Sentimentality didn't weigh on Grayson's heart. His previous second-in-command had been a good soldier, but he hadn't considered him a friend. That didn't mean there would be no repercussions for his death.

In his years of operating the Grayson PMC Services company the colonel had suffered losses—more than he wanted to admit at times—but he'd never dealt with a total unit-wipe. This James Brownstone had embarrassed him by killing his men.

The man had to be handled, and soon.

Most Grayson employees were former Special Forces operators from some of the best units in the world, including AET teams.

What little intelligence they'd been able to stitch together, including a single satellite image, suggested there might have been some heavy magic involved. Brownstone was not normally associated with magic, from what their previous intelligence had indicated.

Unfortunately, they couldn't make out much from the image other than that a single person was killing his men.

He didn't know all the details. The Harriken were obviously holding some of them back, but Brownstone had been involved, and he had been on-scene when all the Grayson men had died. Now the criminals were willing to pay for his death. If someone else had been involved, he could be handled after Brownstone's liquidation.

The gathered men stared at a large television hanging on the wall opposite the colonel, where a blurred battle raged inside a bank. James Brownstone was blasting away with weapons at a man cloaked in flame; the now-deceased Jordan Adams, aka King Pyro.

"Did you see that?" asked Major Tallmadge, the next highest-ranking man left alive in the company. "Those monitors moved, but he wasn't near them. Some sort of magic, I'm guessing. Telekinetic magic, or air magic."

Colonel Grayson nodded. "And Brownstone doesn't seem to have any armor on, but he's not taking much damage from the flame attacks. From what public reports indicate this Adams could generate serious heat. Enough to melt metal, anyway."

Tallmadge's phone beeped. After he answered, a huge frown appeared on his face. "Sergeant Cartwright reports that the Harriken have refused to pay without a body."

The Colonel continued to watch the screen as the bank battle unfolded. A powerful blow from Brownstone sent King Pyro sailing through a front window.

"That's fine," he replied after a few seconds of thought.

The other officers exchanged glances, but it was Major Tallmadge who spoke. "It's *fine*? This asshole killed dozens of our men, and the Harriken are offering us an extra five hundred thousand on top of the existing five hundred thousand if one of our guys takes him out."

Grayson shook his head. "I say we sit back for a while. I don't want any of our remaining men going after Brownstone if he survived. We've lost enough personnel, and we still have a lot of gaps in our intel. We took the original job on without enough intel, and we lost forty men because of it. We need to be more careful this time."

Tallmadge's forehead creased. "Even if we're not sure that this Brownstone is responsible, and the Harriken are using us, all the rumors say he was the one who took down our men. That's hurting our reputation."

"You need to think long-term, Tallmadge, not short-term. Strategically, not just tactically." The colonel tapped the tablet in front of him, halting the video. "Let other people go after the bounty hunter. I don't give a shit if it's Brownstone at this point or some Oriceran fuckers he has in his back pocket on retainer. Someone *will* go after him, and they'll die. It'll bleed out enough of the idiots around here to help us."

"How do you figure?"

"It's just economics, Tallmadge. Supply and demand. Given Brownstone's rep, it's not going to be street punks going after him. If it weren't for our dead men I wouldn't have authorized any strikes at all." Colonel Grayson nodded slowly. "No, we'll let Brownstone thin everyone out. Once he's tired and off-balance, we'll finish him."

He stared at the paused and grainy image of the bounty hunter on the screen.

*You're just a man, Brownstone. You can die like anyone else.*

---

The morning after the complete and utter destruction of his house, James rolled into the parking lot outside a familiar LAPD station. He'd been there countless times, since they performed all high-level bounty processing in the building.

The bounty hunter glanced down at his clothes after he hopped out of his wounded truck. They reeked of smoke and ashes, and he himself smelled like an ashtray. He hadn't bothered to take a shower, and all his other clothes were gone. At least his gray coat had survived.

Shay would be *thrilled.*

He'd thought about standing outside in one of the thunderstorms that were supposed to hit the city, but NOAA updates now suggested they wouldn't arrive as soon as they'd originally predicted.

Several cops eyed him as he entered and strode toward

the front desk. Sergeant Mack stood up from behind his computer and looked James up and down.

"No offense, Brownstone, but you look like complete shit. Did you fall asleep in a ditch yesterday or something?"

"Yeah, of course I look like shit. I got blown up yesterday."

Understanding dawned on the cop's face. He looked down and tapped on his keyboard for a few seconds.

"Damn," Mack exclaimed. "I hadn't looked into it. I mean, I heard about some big-ass explosion in your neighborhood, but I didn't put two and two together. That was *your* house?"

James rubbed the back of his neck. "Look, I was hoping that you guys wouldn't get involved, but you're cops and you're nosy. I figured I should come clean before there's a misunderstanding and good men get hurt."

Mack chuckled. "You definitely need to get clean, that's for sure. But what are you talking about?"

"The gas explosion contributed, sure. But the original cause was the two fucking rockets some bastard put into my house."

"What the fuck, Brownstone?" The cop's face scrunched in confusion. "Are you shitting me?"

James shook his head. "There's a hit on me; at least a half million, Harriken-funded."

Mack whistled. "Damn, Brownstone. When you piss people off, you do it big-time. I don't know if I'm more surprised that it took 'em so long, or that they're too stupid to quit when they're ahead."

"This isn't going to end until I make it clear that I won't put up with any more of their bullshit." The bounty hunter gestured toward the front door. "They busted up my truck, too. *Fuckers.*"

"Look, Brownstone, we can take you into protective custody. Maybe that's the best play."

James snorted. "These people came after me with rocket launchers. If I hide behind some cops, all that's gonna result in is dead cops. I don't want that on my conscience."

"Yeah, but we can't have LA turned into a war zone, and we both know that's what is about to happen."

"Tell that to the Harriken." The bounty hunter shook his head. "I don't want people caught up in my shit, cops or civilians. I'm gonna try and draw these bastards away so I can deal with them my own way. This is all underworld shit, so I'm not gonna hold back or shed any tears for any fuckers who come at me thinking they'll find an easy payday. Fuck them for blowing up my house and messing up my truck. You know how fucking hard it is to find parts for a vintage Ford F-350?"

"Calm down, Brownstone. Calm down." Sergeant Mack let out a long sigh. "I'm not going to say I know everything about you, but I know you're a man who takes a personal slight seriously. I'll pass the word on, but you know this isn't going to make AET happy. Or hell…a lot of the guys in the department."

"My house is a fucking crater." James grunted. "Half of Los Angeles….shit, half of the West Coast will probably be coming for me. The last thing anyone, AET or otherwise, should be doing is getting between me and the fuckers who come after me unless they want to get hurt." He pivoted on his heel and marched toward the door.

"Brownstone," Mack called to him.

James stopped and looked over his shoulder. "What?"

"Don't die, man. You're one of the good ones."

"Don't worry. Even if I do, there'll be a lot fewer pieces of scum in Los Angeles before I go."

# 4

Shay paced in front of the boarding gate, ignoring the annoyed glares of the other passengers. She needed to get back to Los Angeles as soon as possible—hopefully before Brownstone ended up dead.

She sighed. *You fucking moron. Of course you have to get into this kind of bullshit when I'm out of the country.*

Despite their conversation about Alison, she wasn't sure if Brownstone realized how much trouble was bearing down on him.

He'd been mostly on the side of the establishment and the law in the war against crime. The field archaeologist, in contrast, had put in her years on the opposing team.

She suspected she knew how criminal scum ticked a lot better than he did.

*The best solution is a punch to the face.* That was his motto.

Brownstone might be tough and have a lot of experience hunting criminals, but he'd probably gotten too used to them not working together.

Shay had witnessed the vicious beauty of a criminal collective focused on a single goal too many times to underestimate the danger.

Every piece of garbage in Los Angeles would be coming after him, and as tough as he was, he'd slip up without someone to watch his back.

Shay didn't care that she'd seen him take a shotgun blast at point-blank range or that he had some weird-ass Oriceran amulet that probably made him tougher. She'd also seen recordings of him taking on King Pyro, and that made one fact painfully clear.

Whatever James Brownstone was, he could be hurt.

The concerned woman fished out her phone and took a moment to log into a darknet black market forum she had frequented in her killer era. It'd proven useful in the last few days. Brownstone's bounty had become a big topic of interest.

His general bounty had risen to five hundred and fifty thousand, and there had been specific details added since last time she'd checked.

*We wish to make our policy very clear. No body, no bounty. As a minimum, we will accept a head. If you lose the head, you must have at least the torso. These terms are non-negotiable if you wish collection of the reward.*

"Well, that should keep them from trying to blow him up, at least," Shay mumbled to herself. That improved his odds of survival.

She skimmed the rest of the forum's topics. She frowned, realizing she had a money-making opportunity when she spotted some people talking about taking bets paid out in cryptocurrency. From what she saw, it was ten-to-one against Brownstone surviving more than a couple of weeks.

It wouldn't hurt for me to take a little money from the bad guys and save Brownstone's ass at the same time.

Another forum topic caught her attention: *Latest Brownstone Sightings.* Her stomach tightened.

*Brownstone last seen entering the LAPD Police Department. Timestamp, GPS coordinates, and address as follows.*

Shay let out a long sigh and looked at the flight board. "Stay alive, Brownstone. Stay alive."

---

The mechanic eyed the F-350 after closing the hood. "Do you know how hard it is to get parts for this thing? I feel like I'm ripping you off every time you bring it in for maintenance. Just buy a new truck, man!"

James grunted. "I didn't ask how hard or expensive it was. I asked if you could fix it."

"I don't even know how you drove it around with all the damage to the engine." The mechanic moved to a nearby counter to wipe his oil-covered hands on a rag. "You should just sell it for scrap. It'll cost more than it's worth to fix."

"No fucking way. I want it fixed."

"Brownstone, do you understand what I'm getting at? This ain't about rotating the tires and slapping on some new paint. I'm gonna have to replace a lot of shit in this truck, starting with the engine." The mechanic gestured toward the F-350. "Look, you told me not to ask before, but now I'm asking. How did you even get a two-by-four through the window? What the hell happened?"

James shrugged. "My house blew up, and my truck was next to it when it happened. Explosions send shit out. No big mystery."

The other man blinked. "Your house blew up?"

"Yeah. *Boom.*" The bounty hunter mimicked the explosion with his hands.

"Damn. That sucks. I don't even want to know why your house blew up." The mechanic shook his head. "Anyway, don't matter. We're talking roughly thirty thousand to get it back into shape. Like I said, makes more sense to just put that toward a new truck—and the costs might go higher. I'll need a lot of rare parts, and those go for a premium."

James grunted. "Don't worry about the cost. I'm gonna get the people who blew up my house to pay."

---

About fifteen minutes later, the bounty hunter hoofed it away from the shop. Rideshares or cabs presented too much risk of an assassin or a car bomb. He needed to think about his next step now that his truck was handled. At least *something* he cared about was still around.

The bounty hunter surveyed the area as he approached an intersection. A small number of delivery drones and a single police drone hovered in the sky. Cars streamed up and down the road, along with a flowing river of humanity on the sidewalks.

Too many damn people. Too many damn potential casualties. James needed to go somewhere safe, at least for a couple of minutes so he could get his bearings and take care of a few important personal matters.

It didn't matter how badly he wanted to keep his life simple. Preparing for war was always complicated.

The bounty hunter squinted into the distance. Over a dozen flagpoles, each flying a different flag, stood in front of a walled-off building: the local Oriceran consulate.

James had heard that despite locating the consulate in a rougher part of town, crime near the place was all but non-existent. The Oricerans weren't offering much of a presence outside of the consulate, but the fact that they were there had scared off most normal criminals.

Mugging a being who could use magic presented all sorts of unfortunate risks, and no one wanted to push some of the creatures to test the limits of their diplomatic immunity.

It used to be that death was the worst thing that could happen to a criminal. These days, a man could end up a zombie or have his soul sucked out.

Of course, in the end, a consulate was a government building, and thus full of bureaucrats and politicians.

Nothing James had ever heard about Oriceran suggested they were immune to the corruption that had afflicted Earth.

Even their fancy treaty that had kept the peace for years was less about them being more advanced than humans—despite what a lot of them wanted to believe—and more about mutually-assured destruction.

In the end fear kept everyone in line, no matter what planet you were on.

He crossed the street and made his way toward the consulate. He'd thought about holing up in his warehouse, but he didn't want to risk leading his enemies there. Even replacing his house would be easier than replacing a location where he could store his artifacts safely.

James grasped the amulet through his shirt. Given the danger hanging over him, it was all but inevitable that he'd be forced to use the damned thing. The removal of choice annoyed him almost as much as his house being blown up. Almost.

A slick-haired man in an expensive suit eyed James with disdain as he stepped past him.

"Problem, asshole?" the bounty hunter rumbled. He didn't want to pound some random douchebag, but his patience had vanished with his house.

The man snorted and hurried away. "Homeless scum," he muttered under his breath. "We should ship all of you off to Oriceran. I'm sure they could do something useful with you."

"I'm not homeless. My house got blown up, asshole."

James grunted, suddenly realizing that technically it *did* make him homeless.

"Whatever, pal. Stop drinking so much." The man sniffed and picked up his pace.

Yeah, all talk. Fucking coward.

As James continued down the street, he thought about how his life had unfolded so far. He was using his strength to try to slow the darkness and chaos that threatened to swallow the world. Optimism wasn't his motivation.

He wasn't sure if anything would make a difference in the long run, but he couldn't bring himself to lie down and give up. He didn't care if a whole army came for him; he'd fight until the bitter end.

Each step brought him closer to the consulate. No shots rang out. No missiles or fireballs zoomed from above. No angry gods appeared to hurl lightning at him.

That was promising.

Fuck. He'd really let these bastards rattle his cage. He'd need to charge 'em rent if they were gonna live in his head.

James understood the risks of his profession, including how he could die going after bounties, but on some level he'd always believed that if he made it home at the end of the day he'd be okay. The Harriken had put a crack in that belief by killing Leeroy, and now their hit had shattered it completely by taking out his house. At least his truck had survived, albeit barely.

*Sorry, Father McCartney. As I told you, I'm pretty Old-Testament.* He grunted. *An eye for an eye. A tooth for a tooth. A fucking hundred houses for a fucking house.*

*Okay, maybe a little Ragnarok.*

The high consulate walls now loomed over him. A series of concentric concrete barriers protected the gate, preventing truck bombs. A faint glimmer in the air over the walls suggested some sort of magical forcefield surrounded the consulate, which was not all that surprising.

James pulled out his phone, now feeling secure for at least the next few minutes. If any dumbasses showed up and started shooting, ferret ninjas and dragon knights or something like that would appear and deliver the pain. He hoped. It might almost be worth all the trouble.

The bounty hunter quickly dialed, glancing around for suspicious people or drones.

"Hello?" Alison answered. "I didn't know you were going to call."

"Hey, Alison," James replied. The girl's voice soothed his hot blood. "Just wanted to check in with you. Not like I need a special reason, right?" He forced a chuckle.

"Oh, sorry, James. I wasn't saying I was mad or anything. It's just you're always so busy."

The bounty hunter let out a long sigh. "Yeah, sorry about that. I guess that's kind of why I wanted to call." He searched for a plausible lie. The last thing he needed was for the girl to worry about what was going on with him. "I have a lot of meetings this weekend, so I wasn't sure when I'd be able to call."

"'Meetings?'" Alison laughed. "Is that what you call it when you go and kick some bad guy's butt?"

"Well, you know, same difference. It's not like it has to go down that way, but no one ever wants to come quietly. Not my fault." James grunted. He didn't want her to worry about him. "Enough about me. How is everything going with you? You ever make up with Aya over that whole crushed-doll thing?"

Alison sighed. "Yeah, we're good now. I felt so bad. She cried for such a long time."

"Just keep in mind, kid, it was an accident. It wasn't like you meant to sit on the thing."

"I know, but she's got such a pure soul that it's like kicking a puppy or something. I feel like the *worst*."

James smiled, the tension of the hunt disappearing as he talked to the teenager. It'd only been a brief slice of his life, but he'd peeked into a world he could have had in another life; a world with a loving family and simple problems, rather than a world of blood, shadows, and pain.

He shook his head. *I guess the world needs people like me so kids like her can sleep at night without worrying about the real monsters out there. Takes a monster to hunt monsters.*

"Any progress on the magic?" James asked. "I know you've been worried about that shi— Stuff."

"It's the same. A lot of my teachers sitting around going off about my *great potential*, but not much else going on."

"Yeah, well, not that I would know, but I'm guessing these things take time."

A cargo drone dipped low and James tensed, his free hand dropping to one of the holsters inside his coat. When he spotted USPS markings on the side relief spread through him.

The drone zoomed off down the street.

"Are you still going to be able to come next weekend?" Alison asked, a hint of concern in her voice. "Or do you have more *meetings?*"

"Yeah, yeah. Sure thing, kid. As long as I'm still breathing I'll be there." *Big "if" on the breathing thing, though.*

"Okay," Alison replied. "I'm sorry, but I've got to get going. Aya needs my help with something."

"No problem."

"Love you, James," Alison told him and hung up.

James blinked. It still felt strange and foreign when someone said that to him. It was almost as weird as Oriceran magic.

In another life, Alison might have been his daughter. He'd already started thinking of her that way even if he hadn't formally adopted her. Now he wasn't so sure he wasn't setting up the girl for more pain.

He sighed. *You were orphaned before, and you might be again. I'm sorry, kid.*

# 5

James headed away from the consulate after the third glowing butterfly circled him. He didn't know if they were Oricerans or their version of drones, but causing an interplanetary incident wasn't high on his list of ways to make his day go better.

"Keep it simple, stupid" might have been his motto in life, but a close second would be "The best defense is a good offense."

Even though his house had been destroyed, James could still bring more than enough pain to his enemies. He had enough gear on him to launch a decent assault, along with what was in the warehouse if he had to use it.

The main problem was that he'd lose a war of attrition. He couldn't wait for every random hoodlum, thug, and hitman to take their shots one by one. He needed to go to the money source and cut it off.

Most criminals, violent or otherwise, were lazy. No one would risk going after him for free.

Different contacts passed through his mind. He could call the Professor, but he already owed the man for the apartment—and asking him to dig into the Harriken might expose him to danger. Even Smite-Williams wouldn't *always* be able to drunkenly laugh his way out of trouble.

The police might know, but they'd probably insist on putting him in protective custody like Mack suggested. The cops wouldn't stand a chance.

James needed to get the information from someone who would know, but also someone he didn't give a damn about if they ended up being dumped into the ocean missing their head.

He grinned. One good contender popped into his head.

The bounty hunter whipped out his phone and dialed someone he was sure wouldn't be happy to hear from him.

"Hello?" a man answered, suspicion in his voice. "Who is this, and how did you get this number?"

"Hey, Tyler. This is James Brownstone."

"I changed my number just so you wouldn't call me, asshole."

James chuckled. "I've got ways of tracking that shit down. I *am* a bounty hunter, remember?"

Tyler muttered something under his breath. "What do you want, Brownstone? You going to come and bust up my place again?"

"Hey, why are you being so pissy? I paid for all the repairs."

"You're a menace, Brownstone, and now it seems like most everyone agrees. Tough break."

"You mean a bunch of murderous scum have a hard-on thinking they're gonna get rich by taking me down? The

Harriken thought they could scare me before, but that didn't end well for them. Now a lot of people are gonna learn an important lesson about who they shouldn't fuck with."

"I wonder how long all that macho posturing will last, Brownstone. Guess it's good for you to feel the heat." Tyler let out a dark chuckle. "Now you know how all the men and women you've brought in felt. It must feel bad, now that the shoe's on the other foot. Like getting fucked in the ass without the lube, huh?"

James grunted. "I'm glad you're enjoying this, asshole."

"Enjoying it, Brownstone? This is the Super Bowl, the World Series, my birthday, and Christmas all rolled into one. I won't be able to get much sleep until it's over, but after that I'll sleep like a baby, secure in the knowledge that you got fucked over."

"I'm ending this soon." James grunted. "I cleared out the two Harriken bases before, but they've got to have some other local place. I need to know where they are."

Tyler scoffed. "Even if I knew, which I'm not saying I do, why the fuck should I tell you? I'd love it if this Harriken hit ends up taking you down."

"I'll pay you a shitload of money, and then it doesn't matter if I'm dead. You profit either way."

"Oh, you suddenly feeling generous? That's not like you, Brownstone."

"No, I'm feeling angry about some fuckers who blew up my house, and I'm willing to be nice about it." James clenched his teeth, trying his best not to squeeze his phone and break it. "Or I could come over there and have a personal chat with you about the location."

Tyler burst out laughing. "You're going to come to the Black Sun? Yeah, Brownstone, that's smart. You get within three miles of this place, and I'm sure half the underworld would know it. Go ahead. I don't fucking care. It's your funeral." Another snicker followed. "And I will come to your funeral, by the way, so I can piss on your grave. Maybe do a little dance and upload the whole thing to the internet."

James muttered and took his phone away from his ear. He pulled up a secure money transfer app and tapped for a few seconds before bringing the phone back up. "There's half up front. If you give me the location you get the rest. If you're so convinced I'm gonna die, it shouldn't matter if you tell me."

There was silence for several seconds.

"I...see," Tyler said, his voice calmer than before. "You're either feeling generous or desperate, but you know what? I'm a professional and a businessman. Money is money. I'll send you the location in a second, but I've got a little bonus service for you, Brownstone. A little extra bit of info."

"What?"

"This won't be like before. These fuckers know you're coming, know you're desperate, and they have effectively infinite reinforcements. If you go after them you'll die. Your best bet is to hop a plane and go hide out in some fucking hut in the middle of some country no one's ever heard of. Otherwise you're dead, and soon."

James snorted. "That's my fucking problem, Tyler. I hope your dick falls off when you piss on my grave, but if you want that money, send me the damn location before someone kills me." He hung up.

A few seconds later the phone chimed with a text.

---

The bounty hunter's stroll to the nearest car rental place took far longer than he would have liked, but he didn't have much choice. Mass transit would mean mass casualties, and rideshares and taxis couldn't be trusted.

James eyed the rental agent behind the desk. The balding man kept fidgeting as he looked at his computer screen.

"Okay, Mr. Brownstone," the man confirmed. "Your account has been verified." The tone of his voice suggested that he was surprised. Apparently Mr. Douchebag Business Jerk wasn't the only person who thought James was a homeless drifter.

"Good," James replied, his voice even lower than usual.

"Are you sure you want the older model Humvee? We have much better vehicles; brand new vehicles."

"No, the Humvee."

The rental agent sighed. "Okay, and do you want us to fill it up?"

"No, I'll fill it up myself."

"Okay, so what sort of network interfaces are you looking for? Cellular? Satellite?"

James shook his head. "I don't care about any of that shit. I just need the truck."

"GPS?"

"Whatever. Like I said, I don't care."

"Oh. Well, again…are you sure you want an older model? We could give you a newer model with a much better entertainment suite. The model you're asking for doesn't have much other than satellite radio and Bluetooth."

James tightened his hands into fists. He only wanted a damned truck. It was bad enough that he couldn't drive his own, and he didn't need a bunch of complicated garbage.

The rental agent snapped his fingers. "How about extra insurance? Even if you have insurance, it helps to have a little extra. That way you don't have to worry about a lot of paperwork if by whatever small chance you get into an accident."

"Insurance?"

An image of hitmen perforating the Humvee with automatic weapons filled Brownstone's mind. He wondered if insurance would cover the replacement of a vehicle blown up by a rocket launcher.

"Yes." The rental agent smiled. "I'd recommend a good amount. Keep in mind that a heavy storm is moving in. You know how people get when there's a little water on the road."

James nodded. "Yeah, insurance sounds like a good idea."

---

Shay leaned back in her seat, enjoying the comfort and space that came with first class. A first-class ticket on a supersonic flight wasn't cheap, but Brownstone would be paying for it eventually, one way or another.

"Ladies and gentlemen," came a voice over the speaker. "This is Captain Smith. I regret to inform you that we'll have to take a detour to Seattle. Storm activity over the Pacific is unusually severe, and we've received word there may be some sort of magical fluctuations. We'll land in Seattle and wait a few hours, then continue on to Los Angeles. We're sorry for any inconvenience this may cause."

A distinguished-looking older couple in front of Shay exchanged glances.

The woman sniffed disdainfully. "Magical? I told you something like this would happen. Those Oricerans want to ruin our world. I read about it on the internet. It's called 'magiforming.' They're going to make our world more like Oriceran so they can take over and make humanity their slaves."

"You reading those conspiracy sites again?" Her husband shook his head. "I don't think Earth governments will just sit by and let that happen."

"I've read that all the prime ministers and presidents on the planet have been replaced by Oriceran-controlled magical dolls."

"Besides, we've got nuclear weapons. You can't take over a planet with nuclear weapons—I don't care how much magic you have. They're also talking about establishing official magical units in the military. We'll have nukes, planes, tanks, and soldier mages. We've got nothing to fear from the Oricerans. They are centuries behind us in technology."

The woman opened her mouth but didn't say anything. She paled instead, finally realizing a Dwarven woman was sitting across the aisle from them. The Oriceran's mouth quirked in a faint smile and she looked out the window.

*Lot calmer than I would have been,* Shay thought.

The awkward silence that descended over the first-class section forced the tomb raider's attention back to her own concerns. She was racing back to Los Angeles to help Brownstone. Any delay meant the chance of him doing something stupid or dying increased.

"Brownstone," she muttered. "Even trying to come home and save you has to be a pain in the ass."

---

The hitman who liked to call himself "Absolute Zero" smiled under his helmet as he saw Brownstone pull away from the rental lot. He'd expected to have a harder time tracking the man down, but now the target was right in front of him in a normal vehicle, just waiting to die.

Soon the hitman would be half a million dollars richer.

Absolute Zero had heard all sorts of rumors about the bounty hunter. A lot of people claimed he'd killed almost every Harriken in LA and a whole unit from the Grayson company.

The hitman didn't believe any of that shit for a second.

Obviously the Harriken and Grayson had had some sort of falling out that resulted in a lot of casualties and both were trying to save face. Brownstone had probably managed nothing more than killing a couple of high-ranking men and provided a convenient scapegoat.

Sure, the guy could bring in a fancy bounty or two, but that wasn't the same thing as killing dozens of men. Brownstone's only real power was spreading bullshit and having people buy into it.

Absolute Zero knew all about that because he played the same game. A few words here and there to the right people and everyone started believing you had special powers and Oriceran tricks you could use. Then they paid you more, or they didn't mess with you.

The hitman followed the Humvee onto the highway. Brownstone was delivering himself to death. A few surprise bursts from a gun, and the cocky bastard would lose control. Finishing him off while he lay half-dead in the wreckage would be easy.

The hitman grinned. "I'll raise a glass to you during the vacation I take after this, Brownstone."

Absolute Zero's grin vanished as the Humvee jerked off the road onto an embankment.

"Shit." The hitman didn't have his gun out. He wasn't sure how Brownstone had made him.

He pulled onto the embankment after the Humvee, which was now barreling toward an abandoned industrial complex.

The hitman sped up, his engine howling. His motorcycle sped after the other vehicle, which turned a corner between two warehouses. Several seconds later he reached the same area, and he screeched to a halt.

The Humvee had vanished.

"Damn it."

Absolute Zero jerked his head back and forth, looking for some sign of his prey. *You made me. I'll give you credit for that, Brownstone, but you still ran away, which means you're afraid. For a guy who was supposed to have mowed down dozens of men, you seem a little chickenshit to me.*

The hitman shook his head, conceding defeat. He'd track down the target again soon enough.

Absolute Zero turned his bike and headed toward a nearby street. Half a minute of driving brought him to an overpass next to the industrial complex. Movement caught his attention, and he saw the Humvee pull into an old warehouse.

He smiled slowly. *Got you, sonofabitch.*

# 6

Lieutenant Maria Hall took a sip of her coffee, wondering whether she would have preferred to have been on vacation. Chaos was descending on the city, all because of one arrogant bounty hunter. Half a million dollars was enough to convince even an honest man to take a shot at James Brownstone, let alone the vast number of criminal scumbags who populated LA.

Damn it. Why couldn't he have run to Mexico so this crap wasn't LAPD's problem?

The LAPD's Anti-Enhanced Threat teams provided the thin line of protection between civilians and the dangerous terrors that contact with Oriceran had unleashed upon the city, country, and planet. As far as Maria was concerned Brownstone was one of those threats, and he needed to be off the streets.

The AET commander didn't give two shits that all his records claimed he wasn't Oriceran. Even if he was born human, he'd obviously tapped into the same kind of artifacts that half his bounties used. He was the textbook definition of an enhanced threat.

Another of her team members, Sergeant Weber, ran into the break room. "Lieutenant! We've got eyes on Brownstone again."

Maria gulped down the rest of her coffee and rushed out of the room behind the man. Two more members of her team ran down the hall, and all four darted into the drone surveillance command center.

The lieutenant didn't like the eagerness on the faces of her subordinates. Too many people in the LAPD admired Brownstone when they should have been keeping in mind he was nothing but trouble. Once he was out of the picture the city would be safer.

Screens tiled three of the room's walls, each with a feed from an AET drone. They didn't normally have so many active, but with the Great Brownstone Hunt in full swing, no one could complain it wasn't a good use of resources.

There was one larger screen in the center of the wall directly in front of the door. It was currently blank.

Weber slid into a chair in front of a computer and entered a few commands. The center screen lit up with an aerial feed showing Brownstone standing next to a warehouse door, arms crossed like he was waiting for someone.

"Look at him," Weber exclaimed. "You wouldn't know that hundreds of criminals are hunting him at this very moment. Got to respect that."

"No I don't," Maria said. "He's just a cocky sonofabitch." She narrowed her eyes. "What about the biker from earlier?"

Weber gestured to a smaller screen showing a drone

focused on the motorcycle. "He took the long way back. We think he's trying to surprise Brownstone."

The lieutenant turned to the other team members. "Get a team ready to deploy ASAP."

They nodded and ran out of the room and Maria returned her attention to Brownstone.

The bounty hunter glanced in the direction of the cyclist and slipped into the warehouse through a side door. The motorcyclist slowed as he approached the warehouse, pulling out a machine gun pistol.

"The guy should have taken his chances on the highway." The lieutenant scoffed. "I can't believe he thinks he can get close to Brownstone. Stupid idiot. He's playing to Brownstone's strengths."

Maria stared at the screen, not wanting to miss a single detail. She wasn't sure *what* she wanted to happen. She wanted Brownstone off the streets, but just because he was a walking disaster didn't mean she wanted some asshole criminal to kill him.

Justice wasn't the same thing as revenge. That was the big lesson Brownstone needed to learn, and if she had her way she'd be the one to teach it to him.

"What the fuck?" the lieutenant exclaimed.

The door to the warehouse sailed off its hinges and flew straight toward the motorcycle. The hitman managed to get off a single burst from his gun before the collision sent him and his bike to the ground. Pieces of metal shot away from the damaged bike.

Brownstone emerged a moment after with a huge pipe in his hand. He rushed toward the still-stunned motorcyclist and smashed the gun out of his hand. The weapon clattered against the side of the warehouse.

"Oh, damn." Weber winced. "That looked like it hurt."

Maria rolled her eyes. "This isn't a freaking game, Weber."

The sergeant winced again, an abashed look on his face.

Brownstone slammed the pipe into the man's stomach and the criminal flew backward, smashing into the wall of the building. His helmet went flying and he crumpled to the ground holding his stomach.

Maria squinted at the downed man, his face now revealed. "Huh. I think that's Absolute Zero. Didn't even know he was back in the city. Thought he was smarter than to pick such a dangerous target. He's not in Brownstone's league."

"Lot of money on the line. Guess he got greedy."

"True enough."

Brownstone's mouth moved, but the drone's distance made trying to read his lips pointless.

The lieutenant tilted her head, concentrating on the audio from the drone feed.

"There's not a lot of ambient background noise," she told Weber. "Enhance the gain and use the central directional mic. We need to know what he's saying."

"Why not just get closer?"

"We don't want Brownstone to know we've got eyes on him."

"Yes, ma'am." Weber adjusted a few settings.

The background static increased, but they could clearly make out voices now.

"Fuck you, Brownstone!" Absolute Zero groaned.

"Bet them broken ribs hurt like a sonofabitch, huh?" Brownstone asked, kneeling next to the hitman. "You think I didn't know you were following me from the minute I left that place, asshole? I'm almost insulted." The audio feed was muffled and weak, but still understandable.

The other man rolled onto his back. "Nothing personal. Just wanted the money."

"You see, that's the problem. You say this is nothing personal, but it's *very* personal. You're trying to fucking *kill* me." Brownstone shook his head. "I go out of my fucking way to make shit clear to all of you, but you assholes never learn no matter *how* many times I'm forced to teach you the lesson. You ever stop and think about why the Harriken put a hit on me? Didn't you hear the rumors?"

Absolute Zero's face remained tight; the pain evident from his face. "I thought it was bullshit. Smoke you were blowing up all our asses."

Brownstone stood. "Nah. I don't spread rumors that aren't true. You see, if you never lie about who and what you are, you'll always live up to the hype."

Maria snorted. Brownstone brought arrogance to a new level. That was a power in and of itself.

The hitman shook his head, disbelief all over his face. "You're saying those Harriken didn't die in some sort of shoot-out with other gangs or Grayson?"

"Yep." The bounty hunter nodded slowly, then stomped on the motorcyclist's hand; he'd been reaching for the gun. A bloodcurdling scream filled the feed.

Maria winced. "Damn, Brownstone! You could have just kicked the guy's gun out of his hand."

Though if she were being honest with herself, she

would have probably put a bullet into a hitman going for a gun. In this case, Brownstone was being more merciful than AET would have been.

The bounty hunter leaned down. "The Harriken killed my dog because I wouldn't let them kidnap a little girl. Bad shit followed. *You* connect the dots." He shook his head. "I don't like to involve myself in shit that's not a bounty or personal, but lately it seems like a lot of people have decided to *get* me involved. It's really pissing me off. Well, that and the whole blowing-my-house-up thing."

Absolute Zero shook his head. "I had nothing to do with that. I didn't have eyes on you until an hour ago."

Weber looked up at Maria. "Isn't that an admission of multiple counts of murder?"

Maria shook her head. "Nah. The way he worded it doesn't directly implicate him. We'd need something more concrete to tie him to it, especially with homicide looking the other way."

Static filled the feed for a second as Brownstone rested the pipe on his shoulder. "I'm trying to figure out what to do with you. Part of me says I might as well thin the herd a little while you're all so rabid, but that almost seems unfair. I expected entire *teams* to come after me, not one stupid dumbass."

Weber whistled. "You think he's going to kill him? This isn't self-defense anymore. If we get that on the drone feed, there's no way anyone else can cover for him and he'll serve hard time. How many guys at the ultramax do you think Brownstone personally sent there?"

Maria shrugged. "Who the fuck knows? Maybe we'll get lucky. If Brownstone kills the guy, we'll have an APB out on him in minutes. LA isn't his damned kingdom, and it's about time he learns no one's above the law. I'm tired of half this department covering his ass and all but begging to carry his balls around for him."

---

Jiro Ikeda stood behind one of his subordinates at a computer desk staring at the LAPD drone feed being streamed to the monitor.

"Such arrogance." He sneered as he watched Brownstone strut around the downed hitman. Jiro didn't even need to know what the swaggering *oni* was saying to be annoyed. His eyes narrowed. "How long will we be able to access their drone feed like this?"

Ikeda's subordinate shook his head. "We can't be sure, Mr. Ikeda. The last time we slipped malware into the LAPD system it took them weeks to figure it out, so we might have use of these feeds for the entire hunt."

Jiro took a deep breath. "Never assume your enemy will be even more foolish the second time you launch the same attack. We must act on this information as soon as possible. Ensure that someone is on their way to kill Brownstone. For now, let it be someone from outside the organization. They are pawns to be sacrificed. When he grows weak enough, we will move in for the kill."

"Yes, Mr. Ikeda. Right away."

The Harriken leader's attention returned to the monitor. "Savor your victory, Brownstone. You will die soon, and I will amuse myself with thoughts of your fear at the end."

Maria sighed, both disappointed and relieved by what was unfolding on the screen in front of her. Brownstone hadn't killed the hitman. Instead, he'd tied the man up with some cable he'd retrieved from the warehouse.

*Okay, so you're not a complete thug, Brownstone. I'll give you a tiny bit of credit for that, but I'm still going to take you down.*

Weber shook his head. "Guess we don't have anything on him, ma'am."

Brownstone disappeared inside the warehouse after he finished restraining the wounded man, and a moment later a side door flipped open and the Humvee emerged. It stopped, and the bounty hunter hopped out.

"What's he doing now?" Maria asked. "Did he change his mind?" She winced, wondering if Brownstone intended to run the man over, but if that were the case he wouldn't have exited the vehicle.

The bounty hunter looked directly at the drone and waved.

"Damn it, he made us."

"I wonder how long he's known the drone was there," Weber mused.

"Probably the whole time. Maybe he didn't off the guy only because he knew we were watching."

This wasn't over yet. Brownstone was one man, and she had the resources of the entire LAPD.

The bounty hunter flipped the drone off and jumped back in his Humvee, and a moment later the vehicle roared away from the scene.

Something flashed on the monitor in front of Weber.

"What is it now?" the lieutenant asked.

"Brownstone called it in. Even mentioned there's drone evidence of him defending himself against a man with an illegal weapon."

"Damn it. That asshole played us."

Weber shrugged. "We could still bring him in."

Maria shook her head. "For what? Self-defense and leaving the scene? For now, just write it up. I'm sure I'll have a list of crimes and infractions a mile long by the time this is over. We'll wait until we have a rock-solid case to bring that bastard in."

# 7

James found the whole thing with the hitman less frustrating than the battle he had waged to get the fucking Bluetooth in the Humvee synched with his phone after driving away.

Just because he was trying to fend off every hitman in Los Angeles didn't mean he couldn't listen to some barbeque podcasts at the same time.

The next few days and weeks struck him as a good time to get caught up on the latest news. He'd need a way to relax after killing a hitman or fifty.

"Finally," he muttered when the Bluetooth icon appeared on his phone. He tapped a few buttons to initiate the download process for his favorite podcasts.

Not that he had any grills, spices, or recipe books anymore. He couldn't even go buy a new one without risk of the store exploding around him.

When the bastards had destroyed his home, he'd been too distracted to pay attention to the smell. With all those spices burning up, he wondered if the firefighters had gotten a little treat in the end.

He sighed. *Fuck. I don't even know where to get some of those spices anymore. Fuckers. I'm gonna make the Harriken buy me five hundred years' worth of damn spices and some crap made from a rare-ass Oriceran plant that only blooms once every hundred years or whatever.*

James' stomach rumbled. All that thinking about spices and barbecue reminded him of how little he'd eaten that day. Trying not to get assassinated could throw a major wrench into your normal routine, especially for a man like him.

A little barbecue would be nice. It wasn't fun kicking ass and beating people down on an empty stomach. He needed the fuel to fight an entire city, maybe even an entire county.

The bounty hunter glanced at a passing street sign and nodded.

"Oh, that's right."

Phillips Bar-B-Que was close and they took orders for pick-up, which meant that if he timed everything just right he could grab his barbecue without criminals showing up to level the place with zombies or grenades.

Damn, this was annoying.

James took the nearest exit and pulled into a side street to make the call. He didn't want to try to order, dodge bullets, and drive on the 110 at the same time. There was too much traffic on the highway, and there was no way he'd avoid getting innocent people hurt or killed.

His mirror and over-the-shoulder checks didn't reveal any obvious tails, but James assumed another killer would show up soon enough. He'd thought about finishing the previous guy just to make a point, but the LAPD drone had made that too complicated.

And the paperwork.

After the warning he'd received from Sergeant Mack after taking King Pyro down, James knew that despite his respect for and best efforts to reach out to the cops not everyone in the LAPD appreciated what he did. A couple days ago he wouldn't have cared that much, but now with everyone bearing down on him, having extra enemies on the law side of things didn't help.

James pushed the thought out of his head. He'd worry about the LAPD later. They'd been watching and could have come after him, but they hadn't. That meant he still hadn't crossed whatever line they'd set.

It wasn't cop time or hitman ass-kicking time. Now was barbecue time.

He dialed and switched to speakerphone.

"Philips Bar-B-Que," a man answered.

"I want to place an order for pick-up," James rumbled. "Your five-pound special. You still have it, right?"

"Yes, sir... Hey, wait a second! Is that you, Brownstone?"

The bounty hunter wasn't surprised that the man recognized his voice. More than a few people had told him he sounded like an engine giving birth while dying. Most people found the sound memorable.

James considered lying for a moment, but no one who made barbecue that tasty could be truly his enemy. Maybe the Harriken were all secretly expert pit-masters and they'd relax and share a beer together after he killed another fifty of them.

He couldn't lie even if he wanted to since he'd have to pick up the ribs eventually or starve. Maybe the Harriken could win that way.

James sighed. "Yeah, it's me."

"Damn! It's been a while since we last saw you. I was starting to think I'd pissed you off or you'd decided you hated my sauce or something."

"Nah, nothing like that." James grunted. "What can I say? I like to keep busy. Been taking a lot of trips out of the country to deal with bounties, and there are so many pieces of shit hanging out in LA it's like trying to shovel snow in the middle of a blizzard sometimes."

The other man chuckled. "Yeah, I saw on the news how you took down that King Pyro bank robber guy. Good job. You know what, how about this? I'll give you the five pounds for free. Kind of a reward for helping stop that bank robber. Just to let you know the community cares and all that. We appreciate you helping to keep the streets clean. I appreciate what the cops are doing, but we need guys like you to keep people like King Pyro in line."

"You saw all that on the news?"

"Yeah. They had a whole special about it."

"Nobody bothered to ask *me* about it."

"Mostly they just were talking to the cops. The cops talked about how you're a big fancy bounty hunter, and how they don't want regular people approaching high-level bounties. I didn't realize you were such big shit, Brownstone. Class Six? Damn! You're like a walking weapon of mass destruction."

Not that James was surprised that no reporter had dared call him. The last few reporters who'd tried to ambush him for an interview had ended up with broken cameras and mics. Most local media who knew anything about him were smart enough to stay well clear.

He liked spreading his reputation, but only through underworld channels. Media contacts only complicated things. Too much back-scratching.

"I'll pay for another five pounds," James told him. "I'm on a little job at the moment that's going to last a while and I might not be able to stop and eat, so your barbeque is gonna help keep me sane."

"Got a few more assholes to take down?"

"Too many to count."

A loud laugh came over the line. "Yeah, I hear you. You got an Igloo with you? I mean, this is good stuff as always, but it's not going to keep well in that truck of yours."

Irritation flared in James. The stupid rocket launcher attack had destroyed all his coolers, and the reminder of his damaged F-350 didn't help. He wasn't sure if a man could truly love a truck, but he felt something approaching that for his black beauty. Maybe loyalty or respect was more appropriate. Shay had married him to his truck, but he was fairly certain she wasn't a licensed minister.

However, with that woman, who the hell knew?

"I'll pay you if you have a spare cooler I can borrow."

"Nah, don't worry about it. I'll stick some sauce bottles in there, too. You just bring it back whenever you've done kicking ass in the name of truth, barbecue, and the American way. When you bring it back I'll want a picture of you for our celebrity wall, though."

James chuckled. "I'm not a celebrity. I'm just a bounty hunter."

"Hey, you were on the news, weren't you? This is LA. Being newsworthy here is a big deal. I'd rather have you then some airhead actor who goes on about crap they don't know anything about."

"If you want my ugly mug on your wall, that's your choice." James changed lanes. "I'm kind of in a hurry. When I get there, can you just have someone run it out and throw it in the backseat of my Humvee for me? Trust me, it'll be easier for both of us. Throw in an extra charge if you want."

"Sure, no problem. Anything for my celebrity bounty hunter."

James groaned and his friend laughed.

Now more comfortable since he didn't need to split his attention, James prepared to pull back onto the 110. That newfound comfort vanished when he spotted a motorcycle barreling down the street from the opposite direction, going well above the speed limit. Fortunately there weren't any other cars around.

"Uh, I'll be there in about ten minutes to pick up the ribs," the bounty hunter said. "But I've got to get off the phone for now. Don't want to get a distracted-driving ticket."

"Okay. See you soon, then."

James pulled into the inside lane on the four-lane road. The motorcyclist might just be an asshole trying to compensate for a small dick, but it wouldn't hurt to be ready for another hitman. The Humvee was a powerful vehicle, but it was a rental civilian model and lacked any sort of real protection against small-arms fire.

*Huh. Wonder if I should do something about armoring up the*

*F-350? But if I did it wouldn't be the same truck. Fucking Harriken. Now you're making me question my loyal truck!*

The Humvee and motorcycle closed on each other from opposite lanes. One of the rider's hands reached inside his leather jacket.

"Yeah, of course," James muttered. "Here we go, asshole. You should have left well enough alone."

The biker pulled out a pistol a few seconds later, and James threw the wheel over to steer the Humvee into the bike's lane and slammed on his brakes. The rider jerked the bike to the side to avoid the Humvee and Brownstone threw open the drivers-side door, nailing the rider. His bike scraped across the road, leaving a trail of broken plastic and metal behind it.

"Asshole should have come at me in a tank." Brownstone griped.

The biker's gun flew out of reach and James smiled, knowing it'd be obvious to any LAPD spy-in-the-sky.

*See? I'm just defending myself. All nice and legal. I can't help it if dumbasses keep getting hurt when they try to fucking kill me.*

The biker rolled to a stop, his jacket and pants torn and blood on the ground. The man let out a low groan, proving he'd survived. If he hadn't been in a leather jacket and helmet he'd probably be dead.

"It's your lucky day, asshole," James yelled. "I don't have time for your shit because I'm too hungry."

He slammed his door shut and accelerated away. Given that the cops were on his ass almost as much as the criminals, he figured they would come and pick up the latest contestant on *Who Wants to be Beaten Down by Brownstone?*

His stomach rumbled again. "I've got barbecue to pick up."

---

Officer Siad glanced at the computer screen in the center of her dashboard and blinked at the dispatch report. She tapped a few commands, then called dispatch to verify the report. Never could be too sure about what was going on in a city like Los Angeles, especially with all the weirdos who lived here.

"Dispatch, please verify the requested apprehension on Crenshaw and South Vermont. The report mentions gun on scene. Is the shooter still active?"

Her radio crackled to life. "Don't worry, just cuff the suspect and wait for the ambulance. He's already been subdued. He's not just some random idiot, but an idiot who tried to off James Brownstone."

Siad winced. She didn't want to be anywhere near a Brownstone mess. "Is the suspect a level-four or above bounty? If so, I request AET backup."

"Don't worry about it. Don't have an ID, so no known bounty yet, but from what the drone team reports this guy wouldn't even be level-two. Pretty sure he's got more than a few broken bones, so he's not going anywhere. Brownstone did a number on him."

The cop shook her head and chuckled. "He's lucky he's still alive after taking on Brownstone. Okay, I'm about two minutes out."

"We'll tell the drone controllers to announce you're thirty seconds out. That should keep him there until you arrive, not that he's going anywhere anyway. Poor bastard."

"Thanks."

Officer Siad thought, *Nice easy arrest. I guess I should thank you, Brownstone.*

---

"Fuck." The downed biker rolled onto his back and groaned. Pain wracked his body, and he was pretty sure his shoulder and leg were broken.

"Should have stuck to dealing dust," he muttered, trying to crawl toward a nearby fence. "Why the fuck did I think I could do this? Fuck, fuck, fuck."

Five-hundred and fifty thousand dollars was why. Sure, he'd never killed anyone before, but he'd come close, and he figured one little bullet would take him to the big time. Now he had no dead bounty hunter and would end up in the hospital. It would be hard to deal dust from there.

He wasn't a total moron.

It wasn't like he'd thought he could take out Brownstone in a fair fight. He'd just planned to be a chickenshit and ambush him. Tough guys like Brownstone expected big impressive enemies, not low-level dust dealers showing up to pop them.

He should have had surprise on his side.

Instead, the bounty hunter had put him on his ass before he'd managed a single shot. So much for his brilliant ambush.

The biker had been lucky. He'd gotten a text from his cousin, who'd said his brother's friend had told him that the bounty hunter was heading his way. There was no way he could have passed on the opportunity. Not for so much money. Better odds than the lotto.

"At least I'm not dead," the man muttered. "I already made my drop-off with the supplier, so it wasn't like the day could get any worse." He gritted his teeth as a shift in his body sent waves of pain through his shoulder and leg. "*Fuck!*"

Another groan escaped, but this time it wasn't because of the agony.

An LAPD drone that was easily over two feet in diameter descended, red and blue lights flashing above it.

"Attention," came a voice from a speaker in the bottom of the drone. "This is the LAPD. You are under arrest for reckless driving, reckless endangerment, disorderly conduct, brandishing a firearm, and being stupid around Brownstone. A uniformed officer will be on scene in thirty seconds. Do not attempt to flee or resisting arrest will be added to the charges."

"Fucking *Brownstone!*" the man screamed.

# 8

Lieutenant Hall looked at the drone feed from the latest Brownstone encounter and shook her head.

"I can't believe this shit," she spat. "This guy is like a danger magnet. Now, it's like the city should have Brownstone insurance. Covers acts of God and Brownstone."

"I almost feel sorry for some of these guys," Sergeant Weber remarked.

He withered under his lieutenant's glare.

"I said 'almost,'" he squeaked.

"And what's the ETA on the black-and-white arriving to pick up Absolute Zero?" Maria said. "What's taking them so damn long? We going to wait for Brownstone to put six guys in a coma and collect them all at once?"

Weber looked at the screen. "About four more minutes. There were a couple of accidents blocking traffic. Maybe we should have sent a VTOL unit?" He looked over his shoulder at his boss. "For that matter, shouldn't we have sent an ambulance, too? Brownstone fucked him up pretty badly."

"A few broken ribs won't kill a guy like that. And just because Brownstone's a dangerous threat and thug doesn't mean Absolute Zero's a victim. That guy's a stone-cold killer, and he doesn't even try to restrain himself with other assholes like Brownstone." She smacked her fist into her palm. "Nope. I don't want to give that bastard any chance of escaping. The black-and-white can take that killer to the hospital and make sure he doesn't get away. Brownstone did us a favor here, and I'm going to take advantage of it."

Weber stared at her.

"What? Do I have something on my face?"

"No, I just… Do we *really* want to go after Brownstone right now?"

"We're the police. We're here to keep order. The longer Brownstone runs around playing cat and mouse with these killers, the higher the chance that some little girl dies in the crossfire. I don't give a shit that he said he's going to try and draw these guys away. As long as he's in our city his very presence threatens our citizens."

Weber turned back to the screen.

The lieutenant narrowed her eyes as a black Porsche headed straight toward the tied-up hitman. "Now what? Who the hell is that? Is that a plainclothes?"

"No clue." The sergeant shrugged. "I don't know anyone in the department with a car that nice." He entered a few commands. "Our guys are still not on scene, and it's a black-and-white approaching. No unmarked or off-duty vehicles in the area."

Maria pointed toward the screen. "And what's up with his license plate?"

Ribbons of color and distortion danced across the plate, confounding any attempt to read the number.

"Shit," Weber exclaimed. "Plate disruptor. If he's got that, then..." He groaned. "Yeah, he knows we're watching."

"Nothing worse than a smart criminal. Brownstone'd better watch his ass. It seems like the pros are starting to show up."

"Shit, you think he's a friend of Absolute Zero?"

A suited man stepped out of the vehicle with a long butterfly knife in hand. A black hood covered his head.

The lieutenant grimaced. "I'm guessing he's not a friend of our guy. Damn it. Where is that black-and-white?"

The hooded man swaggered over to the tied-up hitman and slit his throat in one smooth motion. The two cops watching winced. The killer wiped the blade off on the dying hitman's shirt before flicking his knife closed and slipping into a pocket.

"Damn, that was cold!" Weber declared. "Why?"

"Because he's an asshole criminal. Don't need more explanation than that."

The hooded man's head turned, and even though they couldn't see his face it was clear he was looking straight at the drone. He reached for a silver bracelet on his left wrist.

"No, no, no," Weber shouted. "Does that asshole know how much that costs?"

"I'm guessing that's the point."

The drone feed died. A few seconds later the computer chimed, and an alert box popped up.

**CRITICAL SYSTEM ERROR IN DRONE 23-ALPHA.**

Lieutenant Hill sighed. *Congratulations, Brownstone. There's now officially someone else out there that's pissed me off more than you have today.*

She rubbed the back of her neck. "Fuck this. We're not going to be able to do this all in-house, and that hooded asshole is already a step above what we've already seen. Time to up our game."

"You want to just gather a strike team and bring in Brownstone?"

"Nope. I want less trouble, not more. We have to be smart about any play we make. Politics and all that shit. We need more resources."

Weber furrowed his brow. "I thought the captain hadn't restricted any asset use?"

"He didn't, but we need more than just drones and guns." Maria nodded, her mind made up. "I'm going to call Delroy Washington in the anti-gang task force. They had their eye on Brownstone anyway, and this is the exact kind of crap they've been worried about. With that hooded bastard killing Absolute Zero, this has gone beyond them hunting Brownstone. As far as I can tell, that asshole bounty hunter might be starting a major war."

---

Esteban smiled as his car drove away from the downed police drone. The Harriken contract on Brownstone would earn him a lot of money, but he cared less about the money than the value to his reputation. Brownstone's name was whispered on the streets like he was a deadly monster. But every monster had a weakness, and Esteban would find it.

When he slew Brownstone, a man who had put the fear of God into an international criminal organization, Esteban would inherit that fear. He almost giggled at the thought.

Strategy could lay waste to any enemy. Brownstone relied on terror and surprise, but Esteban wouldn't let himself be rattled. He'd come close to death countless times. The clarity each incident had carved into his soul made every new encounter that much easier.

If it was his time to meet the Devil, then so be it.

Esteban pulled back onto the highway, thinking of the other hitman he'd just killed. That Brownstone had shown mercy to the others who had attacked him didn't matter. If they died at his hands it'd be less competition, and if Brownstone only restrained them, Esteban's beloved blade El Cid would finish them off.

The world should be made stronger and failures removed from it. That was the way of nature and all of creation. A man who could die at his hands wasn't of any value. Brownstone would die and prove that Esteban was the greater creation.

"Thank you, Señor Brownstone," the assassin whispered to himself, "for finally giving me a challenge worthy of my talents."

Esteban changed lanes. He needed to pick up a few extra tools.

---

James pulled up outside the barbecue place, where a smiling man in a red apron stood outside next to a red and white Igloo cooler. The bounty hunter rolled down his window and gestured to him.

"I'm James Brownstone. I'm here to pick up my food."

"It's an honor to meet you, Mr. Brownstone," the man said. "I've heard a lot about you from the boss. He says you're the King of Barbecue. Says you could run your own barbecue joint if you ever got out of the ass-kicking business."

James grunted. "Eh, I just like barbecue. I'm not so good." He nodded toward the back seat. "Could you put the cooler in there?" He reached over into the back to throw open the door.

"Sure thing." The man picked up the cooler and headed over to the Humvee. He slipped the cooler into the back. "Boss said to give you some plastic bags and drinks. You've got four beers in there and five waters. Not sure which you'll need first." He chuckled. "Guessing you won't want to start with the beers until you're off the road."

"Thanks, I appreciate it. It's been a hell of a last couple of days, so it's nice to get some good food."

"Can't wait to add you to the celebrity wall. Boss-man heard that Nadina will be in town soon, so he's been trying to get her to stop by."

"How's that?"

"He says they used to be regulars on the same barbecue forum. He knew her from before she was on the show."

James laughed. He doubted the championship-winning elf would be eager to stop by a local place because a local pit-master asked, even for a place as good as Phillips.

"You really want an elf to stop by your place and be on your wall?" the bounty hunter asked. "You don't worry that she represents something way different for the future of barbecue? Might scare off customers who are traditionalists."

The man shrugged. "What the hell do I care if an elf is cooking barbecue? It's changed a lot over the years, even on Earth. If we can't agree on what true barbecue is even in *this* country, we don't have a right to say that some elf can't do true barbecue. For all we know, they are closer to the true spirit of barbecue."

James shrugged. "You think? Humans at least share a history and shit. Our differences aren't really that big of a deal, compared to the stuff they've got going on over there."

"It's not like Oriceran is new. From what I've heard it's been in contact with Earth in different ways for thousands of years, so it's really just about uncovered history and stuff. They've influenced stuff in the past, so who is to say what is from Earth or Oriceran?"

"How do you figure?"

"You ever watch that web show *Ancient Oriceran History Secrets*?"

"The one with the guy with the funny hair?" James asked.

"Yeah."

"Not everything he says is true just because he claims it is."

The employee looked around before leaning in. "Just saying he's probably more right than he's wrong. What we believe about the past and shared tradition might not be all that." He tapped his head. "Everyone should be thinking that now."

Brownstone shrugged. "Guess I just never thought of it that way."

James fished some cash out of his wallet. A quick stop at an ATM had netted him a lot of petty cash. With all the bad guys after him he couldn't be sure hackers weren't tracing his bank accounts, so a little physical money might help him stay ahead of his enemies. The ATM hadn't attacked him, so he'd consider the plan a win so far.

"Keep the change," he told the man, giving him some bills. He waved and rolled up his window, wondering if some ancient Oriceran had secretly created the first barbecue recipe.

The guy gave him a hearty wave and headed back into the restaurant.

---

James kept one hand on the wheel while he munched on a rib. He wasn't ready to risk stopping or going to the warehouse or the apartment until he could be sure that no one had eyes on him. The Professor probably wouldn't appreciate his apartment getting blown up.

At this point, the bounty hunter had decided that even the Professor's place might be compromised. The best strategy would be to not stay in a steady place. Hotels with parking garages that would keep his vehicle out of satellite, drone, or easy magical detection range might be a good bet.

*Fuck. I was supposed to be relaxing these last couple days.* He changed lanes. *At least these ribs are good.*

The bounty hunter wiped his hand on a napkin next to his seat and put the bone into an empty plastic bag.

Small-fry losers on motorcycles were easy enough to handle, but it was only a matter of time before some asshole with an artifact or a gunship showed up to take him out. James would make sure that he'd at least take a few bastards with him if he could, but he wouldn't put it past someone to hit him with a missile or a bomb.

The bounty hunter didn't fear death. He only feared his death not mattering. It was one of the reasons he was so good at his job. Before it hadn't mattered, but now he had responsibilities, and something approaching fear crept into his mind. Fear for Alison.

James dialed Shay and activated the speakerphone.

One ring. Two rings. Three rings. Four rings.

"Your call has reached an automated voice mail system. Please leave your message at the beep."

An annoying beep followed.

James sighed. "Hey, Shay, it's me. You know me…I hate to ask anyone for a favor, but I'm trying to be real about how shit might end up in the next few days." He took a deep breath. "Look, don't know if you're really coming back, but if you are, don't come to LA. I'd rather you stayed with Alison until I figure out how to take care of the Harriken and get this hit taken care of. The Harriken know about her, even if they don't know where she is. For all I know, they might still think they can weasel her mother's inheritance out of her.

"Yeah, I know what you're thinking. She's in a magic school surrounded by a bunch of Wizards and Witches who could turn their asses into toads or whatever. I thought she'd be safe there, but now I'm not sure. Maybe it's like in *Raiders of the Lost Ark* where the guy has the sword and Indy just pulls out the gun. You know, like don't bring a magic wand to a gunfight. How many of these magical asshole professors have ever been in a fight? How do I know they don't have some stupid rules about killing bastards who come for them?"

"Anyway, I'd appreciate it if you make sure Alison is okay." James took a deep breath. "And thank you. You make a hell of an aunt."

He'd have to trust that Alison would be taken care of between Shay and the instructors, but he could protect the girl from *any* harm if he could stop the Harriken himself.

Just had to be smart about this. He could take down the Harriken, even if they took him down with them.

# 9

"So *this* is what it feels like to be Oscar the Grouch," James mumbled to himself.

He leaned against a brick wall in an alley as he ate barbecue ribs out of a plastic bag he'd set atop a closed garbage can. "Bet he liked barbecue. Can probably cook up some nice-ass ribs. Wonder what his favorite style is? Kansas City, maybe? He seems like a KC type."

The bounty hunter wasn't certain why he was worrying about the barbecue preferences of Muppets, other than the fact that *Sesame Street* was one of the few shows he'd been allowed to watch at the orphanage; that and old Fifties *Lone Ranger* episodes on DVD.

Father Thomas'd had a soft spot for the show, but mostly he said television was a vast wasteland for the soul.

As an adult, James didn't disagree. He watched barbecue and cooking shows, but not much else. He was mostly busy taking down scum anyway.

What would you really think, Father Thomas? What

about me having to run like a dog because I've stirred the damn hornet's nest? Would you be proud of or disgusted with the man I've become? Do you regret giving your life to save my sorry ass?

James grunted, wondering what other paths he could have taken in life. It was easy to convince himself his strength wasn't a big deal, that it didn't mean anything, but then there was the telekinesis—and that was much harder to explain away.

He didn't use it much. It was weak and almost worthless when he wasn't bonded to his amulet, but even when he used the artifact and his power was strong he didn't like it.

Maybe it was all a way of convincing himself he wasn't a cursed monster carrying Oriceran demon blood in his veins. Being a little tougher or stronger than a normal person was one thing, but moving things with his mind?

That was *clearly* unnatural.

A gun and a good knife worked so he worked with those, but he'd gotten so accustomed to not using his other ability that he rarely even thought of it during major fights. Much like the necklace, James told himself; the less he used the ability, the longer he'd maintain his humanity.

The countdown toward damnation or whatever awaited him ticked faster each day.

"I should have been a priest," he muttered as he nibbled on another rib. "Or a monk. The Trappists specialize in beer. Maybe I could have specialized in barbecue. Started a new order." His eyes darted around, making sure he knew what was going on near him.

Father McCartney always insisted the Lord had granted

him his physical gifts to aid in the fight against evil, but James didn't know. The Devil could give people powers too. Cheap price too: just your eternal soul.

Maybe if Father Thomas hadn't been killed and the bounty hunter hadn't grown up watching the Lone Ranger fighting bad guys he might have enjoyed a quieter, more spiritual life. He listened to what the priests told him, but it was hard to know what anyone really wanted from him.

Live by the sword, die by the sword. And now there were a damned lot of swords chasing after him.

For now, though, James only wanted a few minutes to enjoy his food without having to sit in a cramped seat or being charged extra for a barbeque sauce stain on the upholstery.

He pushed his concerns about his past out of his mind. Enjoying his food should take precedence.

The covered alley he'd found would protect him from satellites, and he'd managed to find a tiny slice of town that didn't have any drones in the sky. Damn rare anymore.

"Pretty good," James mumbled, taking another bite and pondering his next move.

He already knew the location of the Harriken building, but charging right at them would result in every asshole killer in the state converging on him—especially with so many drones looking for him.

Then he would be dealing with both the gangsters and their backups in an area where the risk of collateral damage would be too high.

An explosion in the middle of a major city would guarantee that innocent people died. Father McCartney might talk about forgiveness for any and all sins, but that didn't mean James was going to risk people getting hurt just to save his skin.

Fucking Harriken. If the bastards wanted him so badly, they could have just invited him to show up, and they all could have seen who was left standing at the end. Instead, they had to be chickenshits all the way to the end. Those damn swords were just for show.

James finished the rib and threw the plastic bag in the trash. After quickly wiping his hands with one of the scented wet napkins in the bag, he headed back to his rental Humvee.

He needed to thin the hunting pack, either through attrition or fear.

Maybe if he headed down the 5 to southern Orange County he could lure some hitmen to an area where there would be less risk of collateral damage. Picking off the singletons or small groups would add up, and maybe most of the hitmen would give up. Then he could take the pain directly to the Harriken and finish the crap once and for all.

He also needed more time to think.

The bounty hunter started the Humvee and pulled away out of the alley. He spotted a drone in the distance but didn't know if it was after him.

"Let's see how long it takes for the bastards to find me," he muttered aloud.

Ten minutes. That was all it took for him to spot a tail; some guy in a flashy red late-model Chevy Silverado.

He snorted. *Subtle, asshole.*

A couple more minutes netted him a suspicious drone he was sure was following him. Despite the UPS markings it didn't carry any packages, and it'd been following him for several blocks.

James grunted. "Better to have them all come at me at one time anyway."

---

Detective Delroy Washington stood in the AET command center looking at the various drone feeds on the screen. He had to constantly beg for drone time and resources, and AET had a whole freaking fleet of the damn things.

He resisted glaring at Lieutenant Hall. There were a lot more gang members in LA than enhanced threats.

They were both on the same side, at least temporarily. Delroy had anti-gang informants working the streets to try to discourage anyone from going after Brownstone and identify those who might let their greed exceed their common sense.

"Hey," he called, "put Brownstone's vehicle on the center screen. I want to see something better."

Sergeant Weber complied.

"Shit," Delroy mumbled. "Yeah, looks like he's heading to OC. We should send a warning to them that he's coming, but somehow not tip off the fuckers who are trying to kill him. He's not my favorite guy, but all the assholes trying to kill him are legitimate criminals."

Maria spoke up from behind him. "Brownstone's committed plenty of crimes. Keep that in mind. Don't go fanboying too much over that guy."

"Yeah, yeah, sure. And I'm on your side. I know the

guy's trouble. I'm just saying he doesn't kill whoever gets in front of him like some of these assholes."

Maria nodded. "Anyway, I figured out where he was going, and I've already called the locals and told them to not risk engagement. We'll wait for our chance to take Brownstone down, assuming he doesn't blow up half the county first." She frowned. "That storm's approaching. At least it'll clear out the streets somewhat."

Delroy chuckled. "So now we're depending on the weather to do our jobs?"

"Brownstone's practically a force of nature himself, so use fire to fight fire and all that."

"He hasn't done too much damage so far," Delroy reminded her. "At least, not as much as I would have predicted. We've got to give him credit for doing his best to draw his attackers away from civilians."

Maria snorted. "I don't have to give him *any* credit. If he wasn't so flashy and arrogant we wouldn't have this problem now."

The AET commander glared at the anti-gang task force detective. Delroy just shrugged and looked back at the screen.

He could understand where she was coming from.

Like Maria Hall, he didn't like Brownstone. The man was nothing but trouble, but he appreciated that Brownstone hadn't capped his ass when he'd had the chance. And any honest police officer had to accept that the bounty hunter had helped take down some seriously dangerous men and women who would have otherwise killed cops. Maybe even AET team members.

Back when Delroy first joined the force, the world had

been a different place. The worst threats were terrorists and powerful gangs like MS-13, not dangerous wizards or strange monsters. The problem was, a lot of people didn't want to accept how much the world had changed. He wasn't sure if the lieutenant was one of those people, despite her assignment.

Maria sighed. "As for damage, it's because only dumbasses have hit him so far. What happens when the next fool shows up with a rocket launcher? They aren't going to care about innocent people when half a million is on the line." She frowned. "What if a bunch of enhanced criminals show up? Imagine what a couple of King Pyros might do in a fight with Brownstone! I'm half-afraid a bunch of guys are going to start trouble because they think he's too busy to stop them."

"Then AET can take them down. Isn't that what you do?"

"Yeah, assuming we're not busy dealing with Brownstone at the time."

"Wait, something's not right." Delroy squinted and leaned forward. "What the hell is he driving?"

"A late-model Humvee," Sergeant Weber said. "What's the big deal?"

"Since when does he drive one of those? That guy is practically married to that ancient Ford. When we started our tail I dug deep into vehicles and aliases and crap, and everyone associated him with that truck."

"It got damaged when his house was destroyed," Maria told him. "It's in the shop. The Humvee's a rental."

"A rental?" Delroy whistled. "And he's already banged it up? Hope to fuck he bought some insurance. Sucks to be the insurance company that's gonna have to pay out for that vehicle."

---

James glanced at the driver's door as he drove, glad he'd purchased the extra insurance. It wasn't like he'd planned to take down a biker with his door, but the guy had left a pretty big dent outside and now he had cracks and tears on the inside as well. It'd easily cost more than his deductible to fix.

"They should charge the douchebag who was trying to kill me. Wouldn't've had damage to the door if he hadn't pulled a gun."

James chuckled about how expensive people trying to kill you could get. He usually didn't worry much about money, but he didn't like the idea of having to pay out extra because of a bunch of greedy idiots.

His gaze dipped to the gas gauge, which indicated that the tank was almost empty. He grunted. Every little fucking thing in life right now was conspiring to annoy him.

"Should have let them fill it up after all," James mumbled. *Seemed like I had enough at the time. Guess that's what I get for driving a gas-guzzler, but what was I supposed to do—run away in some tiny glorified-moped electric?*

It'd be fucking hard to lose his tail if he ran out of gas. He could hear what Shay would say if he stopped at a gas station and parked on top of a huge tank of highly flammable liquid.

*Didn't that strike you as a dumbass thing to do, dumbass?*

Every gas station in the county was a fireball waiting to happen right now.

He accelerated, seeing his chance coming up. Traffic was light on the opposite side past a deep median. James gripped the wheel tightly, waiting for his opportunity.

Several cars zoomed by, then there wasn't one for about a hundred feet. He yanked hard on the wheel, sending his vehicle across the median and the opposing lanes. Horns shrieked and the vehicle shook as he passed over rough terrain on his way off the freeway.

He glanced in his rearview mirror. A huge line of cars had trapped the Chevy in the median, but there hadn't been an accident.

Grass and dirt gave way to an actual road, and James turned at the first intersection. After about thirty seconds he yanked a drone jammer out of his pocket. If the stupid storm would just come he wouldn't have to rely on technology. The last couple of days were turning into the most complicated of his life.

James laughed at the absurdity of wanting a huge storm to smack into the area. "Well, everyone will be fine as long as they stay inside."

A quick check out the window revealed several drones in the nearby area, but he only spotted one following him.

"Sorry if anyone's got packages being delivered," James muttered as he activated the drone jammer.

He only had a small number of the one-use directional EMP devices, but he needed to free himself from all nearby tails if he wanted a chance to fuel up without exploding.

Several seconds later half a dozen drones smashed into the ground.

James winced. "Damn. I'll offer to pay for those once this is all over."

---

"I see now why you're keeping your drones so far away," Delroy said, shaking his head. "Maybe we should have someone pick up Chevy Boy there, but damn, did you see that stunt? Brownstone could have caused a ridiculous accident. It's like the asshole thinks this is some old Arnold movie."

"You like the classics there, Washington?" Maria asked. "Or just fond of movies starring former California governors?"

Delroy smiled. "Did Reagan make any badass action movies? If he did, I want to see one."

The woman rolled her eyes.

Delroy shrugged. "Hey, you haven't lived until you've heard someone say, 'If it bleeds, we can kill it.'"

"Brownstone bleeds," the lieutenant muttered. "And there are a lot of people trying to kill *him*."

Sergeant Weber, still sitting at the computer, laughed. "So far the only people bleeding are the guys going after him."

Maria and Delroy glared at him, and he winced…again.

"We'll just add the reckless driving to our punch list of citation." Maria sighed. "I'm guessing that by the time this is over, major car accidents will be the least of our worries."

# 10

"I knew I kept this old thing for something," Tyler rolled a chalkboard out of his storage room in the back into the main room of his bar, the Black Sun. It'd been a long time since he'd felt as satisfied.

He'd enjoyed a delicious combination of petty revenge and professional success throughout his life, and now he would be able to apply it to Brownstone.

The bounty hunter had called him to ask about the Harriken and the money was nice, but the call left the bartender feeling uneasy and irritated because he wasn't profiting from Brownstone's suffering.

Tyler prided himself on his ability to make money in a dangerous world without putting himself in jeopardy. Some of that was accomplished through making himself indispensable, in addition to a assiduously-practiced neutrality. The key, though, was not relying on personal physical threats. He knew that in the end there was always someone tougher, stronger, and more ruthless; a lesson Brownstone was now learning.

Cretinous thugs killed and robbed people for a living. A smart and successful criminal preyed on those who thought they were preying on others while making them think he was doing them a favor. That was winning at life.

And Tyler was a winner.

The problem being, the bartender was having trouble finding any angle to profit from here. The damned bounty hunter was moving around too much so Tyler couldn't make much money selling people his location, but he needed to make money off the situation—if only to prove something to himself and that asshole bounty hunter. He needed to beat James Brownstone.

An earlier chance comment from a drunk laid a seed that had blossomed into a great idea concerning how to make money, confirm his neutrality, and *deliciously* humiliate Brownstone.

The bartender glanced at his new door. The bounty hunter had stomped into his bar and been disrespectful when he was hunting King Pyro. Tyler didn't care if the man had paid to replace the door. He was tired of the bounty hunter strutting around like he was the Prince of Los Angeles.

The Harriken's bounty would humble him and Tyler would needle the man while he was down from the safe confines of his bar.

Tyler set up the chalkboard close to a wall.

The five lowlifes sitting around the bar looked at him, irritation on their drunk faces.

"I need another drink," one of them called. "Where the hell were you? I'm sobering up here, pal."

"Something I want to show you first."

"Is it better than a drink?"

"Oh, it's *much* better than a drink." Tyler nodded toward the chalkboard. "Gentlemen, I trust you've all heard about the predicament of one James Brownstone, the so-called Granite Ghost and preternatural pain in the ass. He's now got a price on his head of five hundred and fifty thousand dollars at this point. I'm sure it will only go up."

"Fuck that bitch," one drunk growled. "I hope they cap his ass by tonight. He thinks he's big shit, but he's just a bounty hunter."

Several other drunks grunted in agreement and a chorus of "Fuck Brownstone!" went up.

"Not saying I disagree." Tyler grinned as he started drawing some columns. "I think everyone reasonable agrees that Brownstone would be better off dead, but the real question is when we think it'll happen. Tonight? Tomorrow? A lot of expert opinions out there."

"I think he'll last a few days," another man remarked. "He's a bitch, but he's a *tough* bitch."

Tyler pointed his chalk at him. "I agree. And let's face it—a lot of people are going to die before this is over. Maybe even some we know. That's a lot of money."

The first drunk nodded. "Yeah, I get that, but half a million ain't no good if you're dead."

Tyler nodded in agreement. "Sure, but what if I told you there was a way to make money off this without having to risk attacking Brownstone? We can't do anything about people getting themselves killed, but it doesn't hurt if we all make a little money at the same time."

All the drunks eyed Tyler, suspicion and disbelief on their faces.

"Plenty of people in the action on this one," Tyler continued, "but maybe we can make it fun and safe for us. That's what I'm proposing to *you* fine gentlemen."

The drunks stared at him, and the first man narrowed his eyes. "And how are you gonna do that?"

"Two things make everything in life better: alcohol and a little skin in the game. And we can all get a little skin in the game by *gambling*."

The drunks nodded slowly, and a bit of interest showed on their faces.

"Let's place some bets, gentlemen." Tyler started scribbling category names in the columns. "I'm going to take bets for a lot of different payouts. How many days before someone wastes his ass? How many people will he kill before he's taken down?" He rushed to the other side of the chalkboard and kept spewing ideas. "How he's going to die? Stab wound? Bullet? Blown up like his fucking house? Maybe something fancy, like an Oriceran artifact? There'll be a little something for everyone."

The second drunk shrugged. "It's not much fun if it's only five of us. Not enough money to make it interesting."

Tyler shook a finger. "Exactly." He tapped his pocket. "Call your friends and get them to come over. Let's make this a party. Hell, I'll go one better to encourage you: half-price drinks for anyone who places a bet."

The first drunk yanked his phone out of his pocket, punched in a number, and put it up to his ear. "Hey, Steve, this is Jay. Get your ass down to the Black Sun. No. I don't care what you're doing tonight. I've got something better. We're gonna have the first Brownstone betting night."

Tyler smiled. "And *last*."

---

Shay yanked her phone out of her pocket and turned it on as she hurried down the LAX jetway. She winced as she spotted the missed call from Brownstone.

"Seriously, Brownstone? You call me when I'm on the plane?" she muttered. "If you died before I get here, I'll go to heaven or hell—wherever you ended up—to kick your stupid dead ass."

She played the message he'd left as she stepped into the boarding gate and let out a sigh, her left hand cradling her forehead.

"You make a hell of an aunt," the message finished.

A few more steps moved Shay away from the stream of disembarking people, and she rubbed the back of her neck as she thought about her next course of action.

Shay had worried before that Brownstone hadn't been taking the threat seriously, but now he was practically giving her his dying wishes over the phone.

Hearing the unflappable killing machine show a hint of vulnerability filled her with an unease she hadn't felt since her days as a professional killer.

*Damn it, Brownstone. Why did you have to make this harder than it already was?*

The field archaeologist hurried toward baggage claim, still trying to decide what the hell she should even do.

Alison was staying in a government-sponsored school filled with strange creatures and people from Earth and Oriceran who could do magic. From what she'd seen when they'd visited, Shay had a hard time believing some hitman could easily get onto the grounds. There was even a spell protecting the gates. All that suggested she go help Brownstone, since he didn't have an entire staff of wizards and witches protecting him.

Of course, a hitman who could use magic was a different matter entirely. Shay sighed as she stepped on an escalator. Even if the hitman didn't have the same power level or skills as the teachers at the school, he still might be able to take them out.

The problem with violence was that people misunderstood what made a dangerous killer versus a victim.

The key wasn't what tool a person used.

Some of the most brutal killers in history hadn't used impressive weapons. The real core of a killer was a ruthless willingness to slay whoever was in front of them, regardless of any pity they might feel for them.

Shay knew that all too well. It was what had made her such an effective killer before she'd walked away from the death-dealing business. Hands, guns, knives, fireplace pokers; she'd used so many different weapons. She doubted a bunch of glorified schoolteachers possessed the killer instinct, even if they could whip a little magic out to impress snarky teens.

If Brownstone made that call he was in over his head, which meant he needed her help. But he'd also asked her to watch Alison, and if he *did* survive, he was going to be pissed that she hadn't listened to him if anything happened to Alison because she hadn't been there to protect her.

A long groan escaped Shay's lips and an airport cop walked over, flashing her a smile.

"Problem, Miss?" His eyes roamed her body, and his pupils widened. He obviously liked what he saw.

Shay resisted the urge to smack him, even though he had it coming. Getting arrested or causing a major incident at LAX wouldn't help Brownstone, and the less attention she drew to herself, the smaller the chance her past would catch up with her.

"I'm fine," she told him through gritted teeth. "Just having some trouble figuring out what to do. You know… personal problem."

The cop nodded, a sympathetic look on his face. "Oh, you know, part of community outreach is listening to citizens' concerns. Maybe it'll help to bounce your dilemma off your friendly boy in blue." He waggled his eyebrows.

Must…resist…urge…to kick this asshole in the crotch.

"Fine," Shay agreed. "Here's my situation: my dumbass friend needs my help, but said dumbass also wants me to go keep an eye on someone important to him. But if I don't go help my dumbass friend, said friend might end up in even more trouble."

The cop blinked. "Uh, okay. What sort of trouble are we talking about?"

Shay resisted the urge to even hint at the truth. "Oh, nothing important. It's just, you know…the past catches up with people. That kind of thing."

The cop nodded and rubbed his chin. "I get it. I've seen this kind of thing before in domestic situations. Let me guess: your friend was sleeping around and she got knocked up? Now she wants you to go smooth it out with her man, huh?"

Shay stared at the cop, both annoyed and surprised at the utter idiocy the man's mind had generated.

She opened her mouth to respond, but couldn't think of anything to say that wouldn't end with her being arrested.

"Uh, okaaayyy," she finally managed.

The cop shrugged. "Look, I don't think you should get in the middle of your friend's personal problems. Really, what you need to do is relax, and let her solve her own problems. You'll both be much better off."

"Huh?"

The cop leaned in. "I'm getting off duty soon. How about we go for a drink? You can take your mind off anyone else. It won't do you any good to sit around all stressed out about someone else's problems when you can't fix them."

Shay rolled her eyes. "Keep dreaming." She smirked. "Unlike most women, I *don't* like a man in uniform."

The cops blinked and frowned. "Whatever." He stormed off in the opposite direction, muttering to himself.

"*Stupido*," Shay hissed under her breath. "You're just lucky you're a cop."

Idiot cop notwithstanding, the conversation had provided her enough time to make her final decision. Brownstone had made the right call. She needed to go to Virginia, both to protect Alison and comfort her in case Brownstone ended up dead.

Shay pulled her phone. "Let's see if the school will accept a little visit."

Esteban drummed his fingers on his steering wheel, a slight frown on his face. He hadn't expected Brownstone to be so bold as to knock out every drone in an area. That'd put him behind schedule, but he had a good idea where the man was going. Orange County.

To the best of his knowledge the bounty hunter didn't maintain any properties there, so it remained unclear whether he was going to stop there or keep going all the way down to San Diego or Mexico.

The hitman chuckled. The fool had picked the wrong sort of vehicle to escape in. Low-profile appeared to be a foreign concept to James Brownstone.

The Humvee was just like Brownstone: large and clumsy. Proper violence required a certain elegance; something Esteban possessed, but a simple thug like Brownstone lacked.

He pulled out his phone to check Brownstone sightings. It was a cruder method of tracking than his personal drone, but it'd have to do. Having everyone in the city looking for the bounty hunter certainly made things easier.

Money changed hands here and there for the reports. An entire temporary economy centered around the tracking and murder of one man had arisen.

He'd even heard of one joker selling t-shirts.

Esteban had already decided the means of the man's death. His background checks and information-gathering had established that Brownstone normally wore some sort of armor that was strong enough to take close-range shots from pistols and shotguns.

The information didn't clarify if the armor was technology-based or magical, but the fool left his head open. The hitman had collected images and video proving that the man could be injured.

He was no immortal. He was just a man like anyone else. His heart pumped red blood.

The fact that a lot of fools—including the Harriken—had had trouble killing Brownstone told Esteban that the local criminal elements were weak. Maybe after he finished off Brownstone he'd cull a few more to make a point.

A nice .50-caliber sniper rifle that sent an armor-piercing bullet to the man's head would finish him. It'd been a long time since he'd used Isabella to finish off someone instead of El Cid. Eagerness clawed at Esteban's mind.

A man needed to show respect for his weapons and tools. If he did, they'd give him the same.

Grenades and rockets were other possibilities, but they lacked the elegance of sniping—though he wasn't above a car bomb if that was what was required. In the end dead was dead, and soon James Brownstone would be dead.

"I'm coming for you, Señor Brownstone," Esteban said. "Make your peace with God."

# 11

The tension gradually left James's muscles as he got farther from the site of his drone massacre. A few new drones had joined the chase, but from what he could tell they belonged to the LAPD. A quiet chuckle escaped his mouth.

The LAPD had been all over him since the beginning, but not a single cop car had gotten close to him. He hadn't been sure if they would heed his warnings, but thus far everything was working out well. The only injuries had been to killers, and the property damage could easily be reimbursed once everything was over.

*Wonder if I can get some sort of insurance to cover this sort of crap in the future?*

James was just starting up his barbecue podcast again when his phone rang. The caller ID surprised him.

"Mack?" he answered. "I haven't killed anyone yet, you know."

The police sergeant laughed. "Yeah, so I've heard. Congrats on that and on not dying so far, Brownstone."

James grunted. "Thanks. I'm not coming in for protective custody, if that's what this is about. And if it's about the drones. I'll pay for them. I just don't have a lot of time to sit around and exchange insurance information at the moment. People keep trying to kill me."

"Yeah, I heard about your little drone stunt. Try to keep that shit minimal, Brownstone. Some drone could be carrying somebody's prescription or something." Mack sighed. "And this isn't about that anyway. Look, you won't come in for protective custody—that's on you—but I and a lot of others appreciate that you came and gave us a head's up about what's going on."

"Okay. I feel like there's a big 'but' coming and it's gonna annoy me."

Mack laughed. "You sound like my wife. Look, truth is, there are a lot of eyes on you right now in the department, especially the gang guys and AET."

James snorted. He'd half-wondered if the two anti-gang task force cops who had been spying on him were involved.

"And?"

"The point is, those eyes are on you because they're waiting for you to fuck up, not because they are going to come in and save your ass if things get too hot."

"Good. That's what I wanted anyway," James said. "I told you I didn't want cops getting caught up in my shit, even asshole cops."

"You that eager to die, Brownstone?"

"Nope. But I figure I'm not gonna be the one dying. Did you call just to tell me the cops will be staying away?"

"Nope," Mack replied. "Even if we're not going to be scrambling units to save your ass, it doesn't mean I can't pass on a little information."

"Confidential police information?"

The cop chuckled. "I think any decent cop wants *less* trouble, not more, so telling somebody about how to avoid trouble is the right move, regardless of the source."

James did a mirror check to look for any obvious tails. Other than the police drones, he didn't spot anyone. "So how do I avoid trouble?"

"There's a hot location ahead of you," the cop said. "At least three suspects are set up in a parking lot right next to an exit. I think they're waiting for you to get close, and they are going to nail you together."

At least the scumbags had finally upped their game.

James grunted. "How do you know they are trouble?"

"Well, the automatic weapons, for one."

"And the cops aren't going to go arrest them?"

The line fell silent for a few moments. "Right now the general party line seems to be that as long as any of these assholes are only focused on you we shouldn't risk going after them and spreading the trouble."

"In other words, the cops are letting a bunch of hitmen wander free because they think either I'll do their jobs for them or the hitmen will take care of me."

"It's not my call, Brownstone," Mack told him, his voice strained. "You know that."

"Yeah, yeah. Just good to know where I stand. I also know most of you have my back, even if AET and the gang guys don't. Doesn't matter. If all they have is three guys I can take 'em."

"Careful, Brownstone. One of them is an elf."

James snorted. "Elves can't take a punch worth a damn. Besides, that's great. More fun. The last two guys were kind of a joke."

"Damn it, Brownstone! Take this shit seriously."

James chuckled. "I'm the one they're trying to kill. Trust me, I'm taking it seriously. Fine, you got a brilliant plan to help me avoid the Three Musketeers?"

"Yeah," Mack replied. "In fact, I do. If you drop off the 5 and head down the 605, you could bypass them and cut back onto the 5 using the 22. Then you could hit the 73 and ride that for a while."

The bounty hunter considered all the roads mentioned and nodded. There were a lot of grassy hills on the 73 where he could take advantage of the Humvee's ability to off-road.

"What kind of cars they driving?" James asked. "Any off-road capability?"

"Nothing fancy, just four-door sedans," Mack told him. "They wouldn't last long off-road."

"No trucks?"

"Nope, not that we've seen. Certainly no Humvee shit, that's for sure."

James nodded, satisfied with the plan. "Okay, Mack, thanks. I'll hit your roads."

"Keep alive, Brownstone."

"Trying to. Talk to you later." James hung up.

He could do this. Three hitmen weren't that impressive,

and he'd fought necromancers and pyromancers. One elf didn't scare him.

These idiots would need to up their game if they wanted to have any chance of taking him out, but that didn't change the fact that every fight slowed him down and gave other people a chance to catch up.

There was only one real problem with the plan. The 73.

*Damn, I hate taking toll roads.*

---

"Remember," Kayla said as she popped a magazine filled with armor-piercing rounds into her rifle. "Brownstone should be here any minute. We'll take out the vehicle first, and then we'll concentrate on the man." The woman finished readying her weapon. "And we're splitting the payout three ways regardless of who makes the final kill. Agreed?"

She glanced at her two companions: one a hulking Russian, the other a lithe elf, both equally deadly.

The killer glanced up the road with a smile on her face.

The onramp had been blocked off for construction, but there were no workers present; only easy-to-avoid cones and signs. The three hitmen could leave their parking lot next to the abandoned Long John Silver's and hit the highway in seconds. It'd be a simple matter of forcing the bounty hunter off the road and then finishing him.

"What if Brownstone kills one of us?" Dmitri asked, strapping on thick gloves covered in glowing runes.

Kayla had no idea where the man had gotten the magical strength-enhancing gloves. When they'd worked together a couple months before he hadn't had them. They would prove very useful in killing Brownstone, who seemed to have a little strength magic of his own.

"We've got a good team," she replied. "We can win this easily, especially since he doesn't know about our trap."

Dmitri shrugged. "This is a man who has killed dozens if not hundreds of people. I would not take him so lightly." He muttered something in Russian.

Kayla snorted. "We've each killed dozens of people, and there are three of us. He's just one man."

"Just saying."

"Hey, you're free to run if you want. I'm happy to take the money all by myself."

Dmitri shrugged. "Just asking. Always better to know beforehand, not after. Less arguing, no?"

Kayla shrugged. "If he takes one of us out it gets split two ways." She grinned at the third hired gun, the elf. "You got a problem with that, Vex?"

The elf snorted. "You're more likely to die than I am, human. I'll enjoy your share." He gave her a feral grin.

Kayla didn't like working with Oricerans, but she couldn't risk that Brownstone didn't have magic on his side that simple bullets and strength couldn't beat. Besides, she'd heard good things about Vex's ability to get things done, and it was always smart to make allies for future difficult kills—even if she wouldn't have to take another job for a while after finishing off Brownstone.

"How far out is he, Vex?" Kayla asked.

Vex opened his mouth and a complex, layered harmony came out. A small glowing orb appeared in front of him with a ghostly image on it. He narrowed his eyes.

"He's not coming," the elf hissed.

Kayla strapped her rifle over her shoulder. "What the fuck? What do you mean he's not coming? He's been coming our way for a while now. Is he dead?" She'd kill whoever took out Brownstone before her.

"Don't you speak your own language, woman?" the elf snapped. He pointed toward the road. "He pulled off the 5. He's on surface streets, but still heading generally south."

Dimitri cursed in Russian and spat on the ground.

Kayla threw open her door. "But you still have eyes on him?"

"Not for long. The coming storm is leaking too much energy. It's making it hard to maintain the spell, but...I think he might be heading to the 605."

"Then let's move," Kayla shouted.

All three hitmen sprinted for their vehicles. Carpooling in pursuit of murder hadn't occurred to them, even if they *were* in California.

---

Esteban smiled as he watched the fools through his binoculars. His three inferiors scrambled into their vehicles, and the smug satisfaction on their faces vanished. The trio had thought they were so clever to set up their little trap, and the disappointment on their faces was delicious.

He'd thought about killing them just to whet Isabella's appetite, but he'd decided against it when the elf had produced his orb. Esteban valued self-improvement, and this would be a useful opportunity for just that.

He was interested to see how Brownstone would

handle a true magic user, not a thug with a toy like the human male of the trio. Witnessing that battle would provide useful information he could apply to future strategies for dealing with magical opponents.

Esteban wondered if waiting would net a higher-value contract. He didn't need the money, but that didn't mean he wouldn't enjoy receiving a higher amount—and the larger the number of his inferior colleagues who perished at Brownstone's hands, the more the Harriken would panic.

He gunned the gas on his Porsche, speeding toward the cars driven by his rivals. The hitman made a point of passing the ugly-ass sedans they drove. No style; no pride in their tools. Wearing suits didn't make them his equals.

"Pathetic," he told them as he passed them. "I'll enjoy watching Brownstone kill you."

---

James' phone notified him of a text and he grabbed it, expecting a message from Sergeant Mack. Instead it was from Shay.

**Okay, dumbass, so I got your message and now I'm on a plane to Virginia, even though I think the girl would be fine there even if I didn't go. I mean, if a school filled with mages can't protect their students, who can?**

**Anyway, you owe me dinner, and not something that involves red-and-white-checkered plastic tablecloths and ironically-named sauces. I want a fancy white cloth with some French-accented snooty asshole who puts a towel over his arm when serving wine.**

James wondered if he should text her back, but decided against it. He was confused as hell about where she actually wanted to go, given that she hadn't seemed to mind the places where they'd eaten before.

If she didn't like the food we were eating she should have just said so. Maybe she wanted steak or something?

James sighed. "Nah. If I ask her about it she'll just call me a dumbass and say I'm trying to piss her off. I guess I'll have to ask the Professor for some ideas."

His confusion over the message and future restaurant choices aside, the text gave him a small amount of comfort. Alison might have been safe with the school staff protecting her, but he was sure she'd be safe with both Shay and the staff protecting her. Any killers would need an army to get through that level of protection.

The bounty hunter could now concentrate completely on delivering beat-down after beat-down to all the assholes coming after him, secure in the knowledge that Alison would be taken care of one way or another. He wasn't planning to die, but he couldn't guarantee he wouldn't.

Then again, if James survived he had another problem.

"Fucking complications," he muttered, passing an orange Volvo. "Now I'm gonna have to learn about restaurant people."

# 12

Trey marched down the street with a half-dozen of his gang following him. They wore their colors proudly and openly, as they wanted everyone to know it wasn't just a gathering of men having fun.

It was a show of both force and respect.

Dark clouds loomed on the horizon. The weather fit the gang leader's mood when he stopped in front of the burned-out remains of what had once been James Brownstone's home. His hands curled into fists.

Disrespect. Pure fucking *disrespect*.

That was what the destruction in front of the gang leader represented. Disrespect of the man who had the neighborhood's back, and disrespect of Trey. No motherfuckers had come in asking for his permission to take out someone important in his hood.

Not that he would have given permission, but at least the bastards should have asked. Instead, they had waltzed right in and had blown up a fucker's home like they owned the hood.

"Yo, Anton," Trey shouted, gesturing to the rubble-filled pit. "You sure you saw our boy get out of there? I ain't never seen a house like that before."

The Harriken bounty suggested that Brownstone was still alive, but Trey needed to be sure. Brownstone being alive would change his reaction, and his decisions would guide the gang.

The other man nodded. "Yeah. He bust out of that burning shit half on fire, like he a demon kicked out of hell. This firefighter was all up in his face about, 'Yo, you gotta go to the hospital' and shit. Brownstone wasn't having any of that shit. He just hopped up in his truck and drove off, and that old sweet-ass ride was all busted up. It had like wood and metal in it. It's like God fired a big-ass shotgun at it, but Brownstone didn't give a fuck because he needed to go give a beat-down. You know what I'm sayin'?"

Trey nodded, satisfied with the answer. "Call the rest of the boys who ain't doing anything. We need to clean this shit up and see if we can find anything of Brownstone's to give back to him. Not that those rocket motherfuckers or the cops left much."

Lachlan snorted. "Why the fuck do we have to clean up that bitch's house? That bitch gonna be dead, if he ain't already. If he's not, I'm thinking maybe *we* should go after him. That's a lot of money. And we help out the Harriken, then maybe they cut us in on some good deals."

The gang leader spun and threw his fist into Lachlan's face, where something crunched loudly. The gangbanger dropped to the ground with blood spurting from his nose.

A chorus of "Damn!" went up from the other gang-bangers.

"What the fuck, Trey?" Lachlan yelled, his hands over his face.

Trey let his hands slowly unfurl and glared at Lachlan. He rested a hand on the grip of his pistol. "Maybe I didn't hear you right, but it sounded like that you were sayin' that we should try and off motherfucking Brownstone to help out a bunch of bitches that don't even live in our hood? But I couldn't be hearing that, because that would be fucking *bullshit*."

"I'm just sayin'…half a million, Trey!" Lachlan grimaced. "Fuck."

"First of all, bitch, Brownstone ain't some motherfucking pussy like you." The gang leader pointed toward the house. "Your bitch ass would be dead if some motherfucker blew your house up with a rocket launcher. But Brownstone walks right out like it ain't no thing. Except now he's pissed, and he's gonna fucking light up all the bitches who go after him, and then he's gonna come back here because this is his fucking hood, where he shows proper respect to those in this hood. So you know what the hood is gonna do back, bitch?"

Lachlan groaned. "I think you broke my nose, man."

"You should be happy I didn't shoot your bitch ass, motherfucker. Talkin' about cappin' Brownstone. What-the-fuck-ever." Trey glanced over his shoulder at his other boys. "We are this hood, and what the hell is the hood gonna do for Brownstone?"

"Have his back," the other gang members said in unison.

"Damn right. Brownstone keeps shit under control.

Fucking Harriken and fucking rocket-launcher bitches. They don't give a fuck about us. They'd leave us to the cops if we did work with them." Trey wiped his bloody knuckles off on his pants. "Now call the rest of the boys. Like I said, we got some motherfucking cleaning up to do."

---

James' phone rang, interrupting his podcast. He grabbed it from the cupholder and glanced down. Unknown number.

*Probably some guy calling to tell me how he's going to kill me, or worse, they want to sell me Amway products.*

"What?" he answered, adding even more gruffness to his voice than usual.

"Um, is this Mr. James Brownstone?" asked a trembling voice on the other end.

*Okay, not exactly a good start to trying to intimidate me.*

"Yeah," he barked. "What about it?"

"Please don't go through Laguna Beach on the 1. I'm seriously begging you here. If you were in front of me I'd be on my hands and knees."

James snorted. "Not saying I'm gonna do that, but why the hell shouldn't I?"

"Um, I'm... Well, without giving you my name, let me note that I am an ad-hoc representative of several of the local homeowners' associations in that area, and we've been informed that you are currently involved in some minor trouble with men of ill repute that is taking you in our general direction."

"Yeah, 'minor trouble.' I like that. What the fuck does this have to do with any HOAs?"

"Well, Mr. Brownstone, if you bring your trouble to our area and things end up...um, well, *destroyed* like your home, as I've been informed, that would have a very negative impact on our property values. You have to understand there are a lot of hard-working people here who have a lot of equity built up in these properties. We haven't done anything to deserve violence or destruction, so I only think it's fair, um, that you...not come here."

He shook his head. "Whatever. I'll avoid blowing up Laguna Beach and/or even going very far in that direction."

The relief in the caller's voice was palpable. "Thank you so very much. I'm so glad that you're such a reasonable gentleman. We really appreciate it, and I'm sure...maybe there's some way we can compensate you?"

James grunted. "I don't need bribes to not blow up innocent people's houses. And I'm gonna be nice and assume *you* are innocent people."

"No, no, no. You misunderstand. This isn't about bribery. It's just about showing our appreciation."

"You really want to show your appreciation?"

"Oh, yes."

James almost laughed at how the man's tone had become even more obsequious. "Then donate to your local orphanage." The bounty hunter hung up. "*I'm* trying *not* to blow any place up," he mumbled. "I can't help it if other people aren't as polite."

---

Maybe people weren't in a toll-paying mood that day or the police had sent out some sort of notice, but for whatever reason traffic on the 73 was between sparse and nonexistent. That worked to James' advantage, as he could cut loose without risking innocent people's lives.

Police drones still trailed him from a distance, but as before no police cars, trucks, or aircraft ventured anywhere near him.

*Just keep your distance until I get this all handled and everyone will be much happier.*

James glanced in his rearview mirror. Three cars were closing on him damned fast. He doubted the average street-racing crew would use the 73.

Must be the guys Mack was talking about. At least these idiots were finally learning and not coming at him one at a time like dumbass cannon-fodder ninjas.

James glanced to either side of him. Steep grassy hills bordered the toll road, and he started plotting escape routes if explosions started going off.

When the bounty hunter pressed his foot down on the accelerator, the Humvee's engine roared and his speedometer climbed. He wondered if the police would decide to make an appearance if he drove triple digits for several miles.

*Probably some asshole traffic cop is keeping a list of fines to make me pay when this is all over.*

One of the three cars, a blue sedan, weaved slightly in the mirror.

*Don't speed if you can't handle it, asshole.*

A second later a rifle barrel poked out of the window.

"Oh." James raised an eyebrow. "That was why."

Several bright muzzle flashes followed, but no bullets hit the Humvee. James jinked hard to the right, then back to the left. Breaking glass flew from the back of the vehicle as a bullet struck the back window.

James rolled down his window and yanked out .45. He kept a tight grip on the wheel with his right hand and blasted away. None of his bullets hit from what he could see, but he'd barely aimed. He cared more about suppression than damage.

"What the fuck?"

A glowing portal appeared several yards in front of him and a fireball blasted through it. He let go of the gun to grab the wheel with both hands. His quick reflexes saved the Humvee from being roasted, the fireball smashing into the ground just a few feet away.

James checked his rearview mirror and laughed. His .45 had embedded itself in the windshield of the blue car.

Fuck this. He wasn't going to win if they could toss fireballs through fucking holes in the sky. Damn Oricerans always had to take shit to the next level.

Flashing lights to the side caught his attention and he glanced that way.

Several police drones hovered in front of an on-ramp with a line of stopped cars behind them.

Good. Keep the roads clear and no one gets hurt.

The bounty hunter's next course correction sent the Humvee up a steep hill and the entire vehicle shook. More bullets ripped through the back and side of the vehicle.

*Really glad I got that insurance now.*

The truck crested the hill and James hit the brakes, skidding to a halt and throwing up dirt and grass. He threw open the door and jumped out of the vehicle, another .45 in hand from a second holster.

The crack of gunfire filled the air and bullets whizzed overhead. Another portal appeared, but the fireball smashed into the ground several yards away from both the vehicle and James.

James dropped and crawled to the top of the hill.

The three cars had parked at the bottom and he spotted the three drivers, who were all wearing suits: a dark-haired woman, a huge brute, and the elf most likely responsible for trying to roast him.

"There he is!" the woman yelled, yanking her rifle up.

James ignored her, instead taking a second to squeeze off two quick shots at the elf. His target cried out and fell backward, blood blossoming from his chest.

*Yeah, should have invested in magic armor, asshole.*

The crack of a rifle sounded and James grunted, pain flaring in his cheek. He rolled backward and touched his face. Blood flowed freely, but the bullet had only skimmed him. An inch more to the side and Rifle Girl would have had a headshot.

*Do I yank off the tab yet? Shit. No. Not yet. With the elf down, I can deal with the others.*

James ran back toward the Humvee. A loud yell got his attention and he jerked around just in time to see the huge brute sailing through the air with his arms in front of him and a glowing blue field surrounding him.

*More damned magic?*

The bounty hunter squeezed off several shots, but none of the impacts did anything more than make the blue field shimmer.

"What the fuck?"

The huge brute landed with a grunt and shook out his

hands. "These work even better than I was told," he remarked in a Russian accent. "Strength comes not just for the blows, but also the legs. They told me the gloves were made by a man who only fought others he could punch. He thought men who used weapons from a distance were cowards. Your gun will be useless."

"You gonna kill me or fucking *talk* me to death?"

The Russian chuckled and raised his gloved fists. "Do you have the balls, James Brownstone, to face me knowing the power I control? I will beat you to death, and you will know the greatest fear you've ever experienced."

James holstered his weapon. If the guy wanted to do a few rounds of boxing, that was fine by him.

"You pissed about your elf buddy? If you go down and take him to the hospital right now he'll probably survive."

The Russian snorted. "I dislike Oricerans. They should stay on their planet. Earth is for humans. You've done us a service. Plus, now we only have to split the bounty two ways."

"That's cold, asshole."

"That is business, little bitch who is about to die."

James chuckled. "And you're using magic. So you hate Oricerans, but you like their toys?"

"Humans create magic too."

"Only because of the crap that's happening with Oriceran."

"You use the tools available for the job." Dmitri lifted his hand and gestured for James to attack him. "Whatever name you use, James Brownstone or Granite Ghost, I don't care. Because today you die."

James sprinted at the Russian and threw a right hook.

The man blocked with ease and returned his own punch. The bounty hunter also blocked, but the blow knocked him back several feet.

He shook out his hands and grunted. It'd been a long time since he'd fought someone who could take one of his punches without any trouble. That complicated things.

"He dead yet, Dmitri?" a female voice called. The dark-haired woman with the rifle crested the hill.

James reacted instantly by going for a throwing knife. The Russian brawler leaped back and brought up his arms, apparently convinced the bounty hunter was attacking him.

The knife struck the woman in the shoulder, and she grunted and dropped the rifle. James sent another throwing knife her way and the hitwoman turned at the last second, managing to avoid being struck in the heart.

James spun back toward Dmitri as the man charged him with his fist pulled back. As the Russian threw his fist the blue field glowed brighter and the punch slammed into the bounty hunter's chest. He grunted as pain spiked from the point of impact. Two more blows followed quickly, then a kick sent James sailing over the top of the hill.

*Maybe I should have used the necklace after all.*

It wasn't the fall that got a man. It was the sudden stop at the end.

James landed hard and grunted, rolling down the steep hill until he lay on the edge of the 73. His arms and ribs ached.

"Not so tough now, are you, Brownstone?" the woman called. She held her left hand against her bloodied shirt and let her right arm, knife still embedded, hang loosely her side. Brownstone hadn't killed her, but she wasn't going to be shooting at him anytime soon.

Dmitri smacked a fist into his gloved palm and the blue field pulsed. "I will be able to take a long vacation after this. Thank you for sharing your information with me, Kayla."

"No problem." The hitwoman sneered at Brownstone. "I'm going to take the next few years off; have some fun down south. Maybe even retire if I get a little investment help. Hey, Dmitri, want to do the honors and finish him off? I would, but that sonofabitch stuck these knives in me."

"Da, Kayla. I will handle him." The Russian grinned. "It is as I told you, Brownstone. Today you die." There was another blue pulse and Dmitri leaped, his arc taking him straight toward James.

# 13

James rolled to the side to dodge the magically-enhanced Russian hitman. He hopped to his feet, doing his best to ignore the pain in his ribs as he backed up.

"Be careful, asshole," he rumbled. "You could really hurt someone doing that."

Dmitri grinned. "Oh, good. I like your spirit. It makes it more satisfying. You're not so tough, huh? All it takes is a little magic to stop you."

"Fuck you." James launched a series of a quick jabs. Dmitri blocked the blows but moved backward. He jerked his knee up and Dmitri staggered from the blow. James thought it only fair to warn him. "You got a few lucky hits in, asshole. You still can walk away, but if you come at me again you're dead."

"Finish his ass, Dmitri," Kayla yelled. She started making her way down the hill. "There are a lot of police drones over there. The cops might already be on their way."

Dmitri swung a meaty fist at James, narrowly missing due to a quick sidestep. The hitman shifted to throw another punch, but James slammed a fist into his stomach. The Russian hissed and stumbled backward.

James had to give it to him. The last time he'd hit a man that hard it'd sent him through a window. He didn't let up, throwing punch after punch, not giving his enemy any opportunity to counterattack. Dmitri blocked each blow and the blue field surrounding him flashed brighter and turned more opaque with each impact.

The bounty hunter pivoted and sent his right elbow toward Dmitri, his left hand going underneath his gray coat.

Dmitri grabbed the elbow and squeezed. Pain shot through James' arm as the Russian started bending it back.

"You fool," the Russian said. "Now I will snap your arm in half like a to—" Dmitri's eyes widened as James shoved a knife into his throat. The wounded man gurgled as he stumbled backward several feet and slowly collapsed to the ground, blood leaking from the wound.

"Hurts, don't it? I figured that might work as long as I was in arm's reach," James told him, "I bet you thought you had a shield against any weapon, not just bullets from far away. That's the problem with magic. Shit's too complicated to be reliable. Too many damn rules to remember." He shook his head and glanced at an angry-looking Kayla. "Do you really want to do this, woman? You're pretty jacked up, but I'm just getting going." He cracked his knuckles to highlight his point.

"Fuck you." The woman narrowed her eyes and dropped to her knees. She then lowered herself to the ground and put her left hand over her head.

"I'm sure retiring in prison will be just as much fun as down south," James told her. "Rent's a lot cheaper, too."

"Very funny, Brownstone."

Sirens howled, and James glanced across the highway. Several police cruisers and drones were rushing from the onramp toward his location.

James rubbed his ribs. Dmitri had given him a workout, but his ribs felt more bruised than broken. It wasn't time to crack out his healing potion just yet. If the bastard hadn't had the magic gloves the whole thing would have been over in seconds.

The police cars screeched to a halt and the officers inside piled out, their guns at the ready but pointed at Kayla and not James. At least his day still had a few nice surprises in store.

One of the cops nodded toward the hitwoman, and an officer moved to cuff her. She hissed in pain as the cops manipulated her wounded arm.

"Hey, not so rough," she exclaimed. "I'm wounded here."

"Yeah, cry me a river." The cop scoffed. "It's crazy how a poor little thing like you got hurt trying to murder a man with the help of two other people."

They forced Kayla to her feet and started marching her toward a police cruiser.

Another cop nodded to Brownstone. "You need to get going. We'll clean this shit up, but these aren't the last guys coming after you."

James looked at the ever-darkening sky. "Yeah, don't I know it! Thanks."

The cop nodded and started toward the criminals' cars. James could only imagine the contraband they held.

"Brownstone," Kayla called over her shoulder. "Nothing personal. It was just business. Just like you with your bounties."

The bounty hunter snorted. "I'll tell you the same thing I told the last guy who said that. Fucking trying to kill me is very personal. You come after me again, you die." He stomped up the hill toward the bullet-riddled Humvee.

No F-350, but it'd been performing well—he'd give it that. He started up the hill, one foot in front of the other.

He sighed. *Still want my own truck back.*

---

Lieutenant Hall sipped some coffee. "That going-up-the-hill stunt *has* to be reckless driving. Make sure we note that, Weber. I'm sure we can find a charge for getting his rental shot up. I mean, come on! It's California."

The sergeant tapped the keyboard. "I'll just type in a note for now, Lieutenant. Man, Brownstone is sure racking up a bunch of citations."

Delroy steepled his fingers. "Can we tag something on him for the knife? It didn't look all that legal. I mean, killing the guy was clearly self-defense. I'm talking about illegal possession, maybe."

Maria nodded. "Maybe, and I like the way you think. Did you see the feed when his coat flipped up a little? The man is a walking arsenal. I'm sure he'll eventually use something illegal, even if the knife wasn't."

The door flew open, and Maria, Delroy, and Sergeant Weber turned to find an angry-looking Sergeant Mack standing in the doorway.

"What the hell are you doing here, Mack?" Delroy said. "Shouldn't you be down in bounty processing?"

Mack snorted. "This shit's gone on long enough."

Maria shrugged and smiled. "I agree. Tell it to Brownstone. He's the one doing the Pied Piper act with every piece of garbage in the area."

"To save cop lives," Mack thundered. "I'm here not to bitch about Brownstone, but to talk some sense into you fools."

Weber and Delroy blinked but didn't respond.

Maria snorted. "That's the problem with all you Brownstone fanboys. You buy into his bullshit. He's not doing this to save cops lives; he's doing this to save his *own* life."

Mack shook his head. "He had his chance to protect his own ass. I told him to go into protective custody when he showed up at the station, and he told me he didn't want cops getting caught up in his shit because he knew it was going to get serious."

"That doesn't prove anything," she argued.

"It proves enough. Why do you hate Brownstone so much, Hall?"

"I'm AET. I deal with enhanced threats, and he's an enhanced threat. Just because the guy bags criminals doesn't mean he's not a threat to innocent people."

"Bullshit. That's not the reason."

The lieutenant arched a brow. "Bullshit? Okay, enlighten me, Sergeant."

Mack pointed at her and then Delroy. "You guys don't like Brownstone because he's doing our jobs for us, and deep down you think that it makes us look weak or some such crap. That guy doesn't have to do what he does. He could have been a thug. Hell, he could have been an accountant, but instead he's trying to make sure cop asses don't go down to guys like King Pyro—and you guys want to send him to an ultramax."

"Do you have a point, Mack?" the lieutenant asked. "Or you just here to whine and fanboy over Brownstone?"

The sergeant frowned. "If you're sick of Brownstone doing our jobs for us, maybe we should start doing them." He pointed toward one of the drone feeds. "Instead of just watching, maybe we should actually *do* something to get this situation under control."

The lieutenant snorted. "I thought Brownstone didn't want us getting involved? What about saving cop lives? You saying we should risk blue lives for Brownstone?"

"I'm saying there's at least shit we can do to put more pressure on the people trying to mess with him, and maybe start convincing the damned criminals they don't get to do whatever they want."

"Like what, exactly?"

Mack turned his narrowed his eyes on Delroy. "Doesn't the gang task force care at all that the Harriken are setting up hits and not even giving a fuck what cops think? It's like they don't think we can do anything to stop them."

Delroy glared at the sergeant. "What are we *supposed* to do?"

"Roust some Harriken, at least. We mess with them a little, it'll give Brownstone more of a chance and send a message to the Harriken that they don't get to do whatever the hell they want. From what I hear, there are a lot of Harriken on the street passing along information."

"That's...*true*," Delroy admitted. "So?"

"If you want your balls back, Washington, earn them." Mack pointed to the feeds. "AET's got the whole county crawling with drones. Start searching for Harriken, and then bust their asses for whatever reason. I'm sure most of them are packing illegal firearms, at least, or violating parole conditions or some shit. They're scum. I'm sure we can find something."

Maria shook her head. "What good does a bunch of arrests that maybe won't stick even do? Aren't we just wasting time?"

"Look, the Harriken started this shit, but eventually Brownstone's going to *end* it. The fewer of them on the street the easier it is for him, whether they're attacking anyone or just paying other people. I'm guessing holding their asses for seventy-two hours will be enough."

A thoughtful look crossed Delroy's face and he pursed his lips. "Maybe."

Maria gritted her teeth. "Delroy, you can't seriously be buying into this crap. Screwing with the Harriken for a few days isn't going to change anything."

"I don't know about that," Delroy countered. "Look, Brownstone's going to do his thing anyway. I don't see why upping the odds of him taking out the Harriken and all their hired help is such a bad idea. We've got intel that Jiro Ikeda is in town, and if he goes down it's going to cripple the Harriken across the entire United States." He stared at Maria. "But we'll need your AET surveillance resources to make this work. Our task force doesn't have enough juice."

The AET lieutenant's face reddened, and she turned away. The three men in the room stared at her, awaiting her response.

"Fine," she grimaced. "But I'm not doing this for Brownstone. I'm doing this because at the end there might be one less criminal organization with power in our area." She held up a finger. "And this doesn't mean that Brownstone's not going to have to pay a fuck-ton of fines when this is over."

---

Esteban smiled at his phone. Everything was going even better than he could have possibly imagined.

"Soon, Isabella, soon."

He'd watched from afar as Brownstone engaged the hapless trio of fools. They hadn't managed to put up much of a fight, and he was a little disappointed that Brownstone had not finished off the woman. The weak needed to be culled, not shown mercy. If it hadn't been for the gaggle of police he would have done the deed himself.

Something more useful came of the fight though: opportunity. With all the damage to Brownstone's vehicle the bounty hunter wouldn't spot the tracker Esteban had fired into it until it was too late. Even through the storm's interference, the hitman could pick up the strong signal.

Pay for the best and you got the best.

Now all Esteban had to do was wait for his opportunity to finish off James Brownstone.

---

Dark clouds covered the entire sky, and sheets of rain fell relentlessly. Lightning flashed, and thunder pealed in the distance.

"Oh, *now* the storm comes," James muttered as the wipers worked in vain to keep his windshield clear. Water infiltrated the back through the broken windshield, but he'd long since given up on the idea that he'd get his deposit back. He only hoped that the insurance he'd opted for would keep him from having to replace the entire vehicle.

Strong winds buffeted the car, and he kept a tight grip on the wheel.

It'd be pretty damn funny if he ended up getting taken out by a traffic accident rather than a hitman.

A certain female's voice entered his thoughts. *Dumbass! And where does that leave Alison?*

The bounty hunter hadn't spotted any tails for a while, or drones for that matter. The weather was more than enough to keep the technological spies-in-the-sky off him, and from what he'd heard on the radio there was more than a little magical energy in the storm. He could only hope that might keep any magical spying off his ass as well.

"I need a fucking break," James griped. He wanted to eat a little more barbecue.

He'd worried that the hitmen might have shot up his Igloo, but there was no bullet damage to the cooler or its precious barbeque cargo. At least one thing had gone his way.

The storm provided the cover he needed. The lack of surveillance meant he had a chance to find a place to rest for the night while he recovered from his fight with Dmitri and figured out the next part of his plan.

The quality of the killers had gone up only slightly and the numbers were only a bit higher. He needed to find some way to get them to come at him all at once so he could finish off the Harriken's Rent-an-Army and then go handle the gangsters directly without having to watch his back.

James squinted into the rain. Visibility was almost non-existent, but he did spot an exit sign that said gas and lodging coming up.

"Time to rest."

# 14

Thank God for underground parking, James thought as the elevator dinged and he pulled his suitcase filled with gear from the car. The Igloo rested precariously on top.

His room wasn't that far from the elevator, so he managed to get everything to the room without incident. The last thing he needed was to spill any of his food.

"Next time I'll ask to borrow a cooler with wheels," James muttered as he slid his keycard into the lock. The door clicked and he pulled everything inside.

Getting a room at the hotel had required some quick thinking on James' part. The best lies always contained a core of truth, so he'd explained the obvious damage to his vehicle by discussing how some ruthless criminals had tried to pull him over on the highway, which he attributed to an attempted carjacking. He claimed he'd fled and lost them, but now was too afraid to go back home.

The shocked and gullible front desk clerk had called the police; specifically Sergeant Mack, at James' suggestion. After a quick conversation with James, the sergeant had promptly told the clerk to not worry about the situation and that the police were aware of what had happened.

With that taken care of, the bounty hunter finished registering for a room under the fake name of Thomas McCartney and parked the Humvee in the hotel's underground parking garage. It would keep his vehicle out of sight of any drones or satellites even if the weather cleared.

James still wasn't sure if or how much the storm would protect him from magical detection, but he'd already taken on an elf and a human using an artifact and survived, so he was worried less about that issue than his building or vehicle being blown up by a rocket launcher.

Now safely in a room for the night, James had to decide on his next move. The key to finishing the manhunt would be to pick off as many hitmen as he could using a few flashy displays of ultraviolence, but that would require somewhere he could really let loose. Maybe even cause a few explosions of his own.

He pulled up a map of Southern California on his phone to try to plot out his driving route and possible locations for the showdown.

James caught sight a possibility. "Coto de Caza."

It was a good start. The security associated with the private gated community had increased in recent decades, and James could pass through there to get to private land where a few explosions wouldn't hurt—with appropriate compensation provided afterward.

Their security wouldn't stop any halfway-decent professional killer, but it'd assure that no random fools would continue following him. Once the big fish had been taken out, the losers—like the first two men who had gone after him that day—would give up and then he could take it to the Harriken.

James scrolled a bit farther down the map and nodded as a plan crystallized. "Yeah, this could work. This could work really well. Just need a few things to make it happen."

James swiped to his contacts list and placed a call to the Professor.

"Hello, lad," the older man answered. "You're still breathing. I'm proud of you. Many good men would already be dead by now."

The bounty hunter chuckled. "I'm trying."

"I also appreciate that my little loan didn't backfire horribly on me."

"What, you were expecting someone to blow your apartment up with a rocket launcher?"

The Professor laughed. "Yes, actually. You do have a way of attracting trouble."

"Well, since that went so well I'm gonna need another favor. Two, actually. I need to ask you about some things."

---

Esteban adjusted his binoculars. Despite the poor visibility due to the weather, he was sure no vehicles had left the parking garage since Brownstone's Humvee had entered.

The bounty hunter had obviously holed up for the

night. Esteban doubted anyone else even knew the man was there. It could be an excellent opportunity to take him out.

The hitman sucked in a breath and slowly let it out. The tactical situation favored Brownstone. Even if the man thought he was somewhat safe, he probably still had numerous weapons with him and might be half-expecting a raid on his room. And getting the location of the room might not be easy either, depending on the systems and staff.

The hitman might have put a tracker on the vehicle, but he had no way of knowing where in the hotel his quarry was. Esteban still had surprise on his side, but that could be lost if he bumbled around seeking Brownstone.

The narrow hallways and small rooms favored the bounty hunter, and the hitman did want to give Isabella her chance to taste blood again. It was only fair, since it'd been a while.

Esteban shook his head. No. Taking on Brownstone tonight played to the thug's strength, not his. More importantly, Brownstone hadn't ditched the Humvee, which meant it'd be trivial to pick up his trail the next day.

Tomorrow the hitman would end it. He rubbed his chin, falling even deeper into thought as he turned away.

*I might need to remove the head for easier transport. I should go buy a cleaver and a cooler.*

---

Shay stared down at the sleeping Alison. The field archaeologist knew she should get some rest herself, but she was still wired from the change of travel plans, worry over Brownstone, and the two hours of chattering about the school.

Shay now knew far too much about the various social cliques at the school.

She chuckled quietly. It might have been a school where kids were learning to harness powerful magic, but in the end they were still kids and more obsessed with the here and now than their post-education future.

Good. The future wasn't always pleasant.

Alison's phone rang and Shay rushed over to grab it. She hurried into the bathroom, closed the door, and answered the call.

"Alison, I hope it's not too late," Brownstone's deep voice began. "I figured I'd call as soon as I got a chance, and it's just...been a busy day."

"It's me," Shay told him. "Alison's asleep."

"Shay? You're there already?"

"Been here for a while. Spent hours talking about...a lot of stuff." Shay chuckled. "When she spent time around me before she wasn't as comfortable with me, but now that I'm 'Aunt Shay' it's nonstop. I had no idea teenage girls talked so much."

Silence choked the line for a second before Brownstone replied, "I guess we both had rough childhoods in our own ways. I don't always think about that with you."

Shay sighed. "Don't get all weepy on me now; it's not very attractive. Yeah, my teenage life was different and difficult, but it's not something I normally spend a lot of time worrying about. And hell...Alison's dad sold her mom to gangsters and tried to sell her too, so it hadn't all been peaches and cream for her. As for me, mostly I just try and ignore my past."

"Probably a good idea, if you say so."

"I do say so."

Brownstone grunted. "Anyway, how is Alison doing?"

"She's fine. The headmistress all but laughed at me over the idea of Alison being in danger here, but they are still letting me stay. I've...kind of tried to downplay what's going on in LA, but it doesn't help that the kid can go on the net and read the news claiming a major gang war is going on, and your name keeps popping up in association with it."

"Gang war? They're all coming after me, but it's not really a war." Brownstone chuckled. "More like a scrimmage. What about you? I hope you didn't run away from something too important."

"It wasn't a big deal. I was on the job in Japan. There was supposed to be an artifact at an abandoned shrine in Hokkaido: an Ainu sacred carving."

"Ainu?"

"Indigenous people in Hokkaido. Anyway, when I got there the site was pretty much a crater, but I do have a good lead on where to find it after I'm done with the babysitting gig."

Brownstone grunted. "Sounds more interesting than my last few days of people trying to kill me."

"Anyone hurt you? Even *you* get banged up."

"Not much. Just scratched up a little." Shay could practically hear the shrug.

She frowned into the mirror as if Brownstone could see her expression somehow. "Do you have any sort of plan for ending this?"

"Yeah, I've got something in the works. It'll at least get the freelancers off my ass, and then I'll figure out how to deal with the people writing the checks." Brownstone cleared his throat. "Look, Shay...um, I just wanted to say thanks for coming back early, and thanks for going to Virginia. Knowing you're there watching out for Alison lets me feel a lot better about everything that's going on, and I'm happy to pay you back with towel-wearing waiters and all that."

Shay blinked at her phone and bit down on a laugh. His idea was close enough to what she wanted, and she saw no reason to spin up an already stressed-out man by correcting him. "You're welcome, Brownstone."

The rustle of Alison shifting in bed caught Shay's attention.

"Okay, I think I better go. Stay alive."

"I'm trying. Talk to you later." Brownstone hung up.

Shay shook her head, thinking about the towel-wearing-waiter thing.

"You're the real deal when it comes to raw material," she muttered. "Grade-A material, but it's still damn raw."

Shay glanced down at Alison, who'd shifted under her blankets.

*So this is what it means to care. It doesn't hurt as much as I thought it would.*

Tyler went over to the chalkboard, carefully navigating through the throng of people choking his bar. He had a hard time remembering a time when his place had been as busy. Between the drinks and the bets, he was making a killing. It almost made him want to give up the information-broker business.

He picked up a piece of chalk and the riotous din quieted.

"Now, not sure how many of you know this, but three more people went after Brownstone today. My contacts just let me know that two of them were killed; an elf and a human who was using a magical artifact. On top of it, Kayla Malone was injured and arrested." Tyler erased a few numbers on the board and started writing in new odds. "So, with the action today, we can definitely see the odds of magic being used for the final kill going up. And too bad for the suckers who bet that Brownstone would make it through the day, let alone the whole hunt, without killing anyone."

The crowd erupted in laughter and a few men jumped out of their seats and pushed their way toward the exits. Tyler didn't care. He had their money and more than enough other customers.

The bartender tapped the chalk against the top of the board. "But for you people who laid down bets on whether Brownstone would die on the first day of betting, don't worry; we still have several more hours today, and just so you know, if that little bitch runs to a different time zone we're still using local time. If you want to make any more bets, I'll be at the bar."

A huge bear of a man sitting at a table waved at Tyler.

"I'll put down a hundred that he'll get axed tonight. I like the long odds. Great payoff." He reached into his wallet to pull out the bills and handed them to the bartender. He glanced at the board. "You're making a lot of money, Tyler."

"Hey, what can I say? It pays to be the house."

"What are you going to do with all the money?" asked another lowlife.

"Who the fuck knows? Maybe I'll use it to renovate a bit. That would be the ultimate irony. I'll use the money from Brownstone's hit to make this place nicer."

The huge man laughed. "Yeah, that would be funny." He slapped a hand down on the table. "Maybe get some tables that don't look like some shit you picked up at a half-price sale."

Another man gestured to a cracked wall. "It's called 'paint,' Tyler. They invented it even before the Oriceran shit happened."

A woman at the bar giggled. "Your bathroom is so disgusting that I'm wondering if it's haunted."

Tyler let out a strained laugh. "Yeah, lots of work to do."

He managed not to curl his hands into fists as he headed back to the bar, despite how hot his face was. All these maggots had freely come to his place. They didn't have the right to criticize his bar and act like it was trashy.

It wasn't like he wanted it to be. The whole point was to maintain a certain comfort level for the regular clientele, who happened to be bottom-feeding criminals.

*Maybe if I made this place nicer I wouldn't have to cater to lowlifes.*

"Give me another beer, Tyler," a man with bloodshot

eyes ordered. He was sitting at the bar. He laughed. "You know, there *is* one nice thing in the bar. *Really* nice."

Tyler started pouring the man's beer. "What's that?"

The man pointed toward the door. "That new door Brownstone bought after destroying the last one." He burst into laughter and half the bar joined him.

15

James pulled the Humvee up to the security gate in Coto de Caza with a forced smile on his face. The security guard in the gatehouse eyed him with suspicion and opened his window, one hand resting on his gun.

*What? Is it my shabby gray coat? My bullet-riddled vehicle? Come on, just because you can judge this book by its cover doesn't mean you should. Or at least I need you not to today.*

He resisted the urge to snort at the man's ready posture. He doubted the guard had ever had to deal with a serious threat. A hitman would have shot him already.

"Are you sure you're in the right place, sir?" the guard asked. "This is a very exclusive community, and no solicitation is permitted."

"Yes," James replied. "Unfortunately I ran into some people who thought they could use the cover of the storm to try and take my vehicle. You know, kids these days. I blame all those Oricerans."

"Okay…and you decided to come to Coto instead of going to the police because…"

"Major business meetings can't be rescheduled that easily," James informed him, the lie coming almost effortlessly—even though he was annoyed at having to lie. "I've been trying to get this meeting to happen for months, and my business contact isn't a man I can easily schedule time with."

James resisted the urge to glare or grunt. Even if he didn't look the part of a rich business jerk, he knew confidence could bluff him through the gates. Hell, this was Southern California, not New York. A billionaire might be in a hoody and a t-shirt with a video-game character on it.

The other man's gaze traveled from James to the back window before returning to the bounty hunter. "I…see."

James shook his head. "Anyway, I'm here to meet with Professor Smite-Williams at the golf club for the aforementioned business meeting. I'm Thomas McCartney. I can give you a number to call if you need to verify the meeting."

*I hope you set this shit up beforehand, Professor. I don't want to have to knock out some innocent security jerk to make this happen.*

"If he's registered for the meeting, that shouldn't be necessary." The guard glanced down at his computer, tapped away for a few moments, then looked back at James with disapproval on his face. "Yes, Professor Smite-Williams did let us know you'd be coming, Mr. McCartney." The guard reached into a drawer and pulled out a guest pass. "Have you contacted the police about your vehicle, sir?"

"Yes. They told me there's nothing they can really do until the storm's over, and I didn't dare delay this meeting. Can't risk getting fired, you know. This is a major client."

"I'm sorry you had to go through that." The guard nodded, a sympathetic look finally appearing on his face. "Well, no scum gets through here, so rest assured, there'll be no incidents during your time in Coto de Caza."

*No scum? Do I count?*

"That's good to know," James replied with an even broader fake smile. His face hurt. He placed the guest pass on the dashboard. "It's been a rough couple of days, you know?"

"I'm sure." The guard pressed a button and the gate slid open with a hum.

James pulled the damaged Humvee through. He didn't like lying and misrepresenting his identity. The more lies a man told the more he had to keep track of, and that led to straightforward things turning complicated.

That was one of the reasons he enjoyed bounty hunting. He didn't have to rely on misdirection or fibs. He tracked people, found them, and brought them in. Simple as a straight line, most days.

*Fucking Harriken. I sent my message to you and I figured you got it, but nah. You obviously need a reminder. Fine. Once I've cleared out the riffraff I'm coming straight for you, and I won't stop even if the cops tell me to lay off.*

The damaged Humvee maneuvered through the local streets. Heavy rain still fell from the sky, but the thunder and lightning had ceased for the moment. James kept his speed low, not wanting to accidentally nail some stupid kid who decided to play in the street on a rainy day.

Or worse yet, get a stupid speeding ticket. That would make it easier for those tracking him. He could hear it now.

*Where's James Brownstone?*

*By the car flashing the blue and red lights, properly kissing that cop's ass.*

He looked around as he drove. The term "gated community" was insufficient to properly capture the scale of Coto de Caza. James' review of the map had indicated that the community was seven miles long and a couple of miles wide.

A damned city unto itself.

His destination was the eastern edge of the community, an area which would allow him easy access to mostly private hilly terrain. It was a great place to gather hitmen and lead them to their dooms without random buildings getting destroyed. First, though, he needed a few tools to implement his plan, and that required the Professor.

James made it through the main community and headed in the general direction of Crow Canyon on a back road. After a few more minutes of driving, he spotted a bright red Jaguar parked on the side of the road. The bounty hunter pulled over and threw open his passenger-side door.

The Professor hurried out of the Jaguar in a ridiculous yellow rain poncho that made him look like some sort of kid waiting for his school bus. He pulled himself into the passenger seat and shut the door, a small briefcase in hand.

"If I wanted this much rain I would have moved to Seattle," the Professor whined.

"Thanks for agreeing to help me out, Professor," James

told him. "This will make things a lot easier. I think I'll be able to finish off all these hitmen with the plan I outlined over the phone."

The Professor handed him the briefcase. "I hope you know what you're doing, lad, because it sounds to me like you have to get a lot of things going your way for that plan to work—and I don't know if you're that lucky. The fact that you're being chased by a bunch of hitmen suggests you're not."

James shrugged. "It's not luck if you're cheating a little."

The Professor chuckled. "Aye, lad." He patted the briefcase. "Both of the items you requested are inside. Note, I'm *loaning* them to you, not *giving* them to you. You already owe me a few favors, and if you destroy these we might have to bring back indentured servitude."

The bounty hunter grunted, then a chuckle escaped his lips. "Thanks. I'll keep that in mind and make sure not to break them."

The older man eyed James severely, but it was hard to take him seriously in the rain poncho. James managed not to laugh, but only barely.

"The first item you requested will work for five minutes. The other...two minutes if you're lucky, but I wouldn't push it past a minute to be safe."

"Okay."

Smite-Williams stared at James for a few long seconds. "Don't die, lad. I like to collect on my debts."

James looked at the Professor. "I'm not going to die. Not for a few days, anyway."

The Professor opened the door, hopped out, and hurried back into his Jaguar. A moment later, the car disappeared down the road. James started up his damaged Humvee and continued toward his ultimate destination.

The only major disadvantage to his plan was that he'd be forced to ditch the vehicle—and be forced to pay for it—but given the level of damage it'd already sustained James had resigned himself to that fate. He only hoped insurance would cushion the blow.

"Gonna have to hunt a few high-level bounties after this," James muttered, "to make up for all this money I'll be shelling out. Maybe I should sue the Harriken. It'd be funny to see how they'd react to that shit."

The Humvee rattled and shook as James headed off the road toward the hilly country, which was dominated by grass and trails. The trees grew sparser, but that didn't matter. He hadn't come to this area to hide.

Being spotted was a major part of the plan. He needed his enemy to have at least *some* clue where he was if the plan was going to work.

When James finally brought the vehicle to a halt he glanced into the backseat at the Igloo and sighed. Just another thing he'd have to replace. It wasn't like he could hike at the speed he needed and tow a cooler along with him.

He reached into the back and unzipped his go-case. It was time to make a more portable go-bag. He pulled a collapsible backpack out of the case and started loading gear from the suitcase into it. While he hoped to have everything resolved in the next day or two, he wanted to be prepared if things took longer.

"Glad I stuck a hat in here," James mumbled to himself as

he listened to the rain pound against the roof and windows. "Maybe I should have brought a stupid-looking poncho, too. Bet Shay would have loved that. Would have gone on about my fashion sense for a whole fucking five minutes."

A few Ziploc bags filled with ice and ribs were deposited into the backpack, along with some bottles of water. It'd have to do for a meal on the run, and it wasn't like he couldn't go a day without food if needed.

James grabbed a bottle of beer. It wouldn't hurt to have one before he started his plan.

He twisted the top off and raised it in a toast. *Cheers to me and all the assholes I'm about to take down.*

---

Shay sat on the edge of the bed as she waited for Alison to emerge from her morning shower. They hadn't talked much about Brownstone the night before, and now she was considering lying to the girl and claiming that he really wasn't in that much danger despite what she might have heard on the news. It didn't seem fair that Alison should have to worry about the bounty hunter, especially when there was nothing she could do to help him.

The teen emerged from the bathroom in a robe, her hair still wet.

"Look, Alison," Shay said. "I think I should be a little more honest about what's going on with Brownstone. I kind of gave you a line about what was going on, but that's not really the whole truth. I thought about lying to protect you, but I think—"

"You shouldn't lie to me," Alison told her, tilting her head.

Shay held up a hand. "Yeah, yeah, I know. Lying's bad and all that. Like I said, I *thought* about it, but I decided against it. After everything you've gone through, you deserve to know when bad things are happening so you can figure out how you want to deal with them your own way."

The girl shook her head. "No, you don't understand, Aunt Shay. You shouldn't lie to me because I've learned a few things...and well, I can tell when people are lying to me now. Most of the time, anyway. I knew last night that you were holding something back, and I hoped you'd tell me the truth eventually."

Shay blinked. "You can tell when people are lying? That's...handy. That's *very* handy."

Alison smiled and sat beside Shay. "I'm glad you decided to treat me like an adult, though. I kind of figured James was in more trouble anyway, just because you're here and all." She sighed. "I've been trying to not pay attention to anything negative going on in LA. It's kind of easy here. We're like in our own world, but I still worry about James."

"I don't know if it's possible for Brownstone to ever *not* be in trouble, but this is kind of bigger than normal." Shay stood and started pacing. "Look, the truth is that there's no gang war going on in LA. That's just a line the police are feeding people so they can look like they have control of the situation. The truth is, there are a lot of people looking to kill Brownstone right now." She winced. "More than the quantity he normally pisses off."

"Why are so many people trying to kill James? I mean, why more than normal?"

Shay looked away, the urge to lie rising again. Dealing with a teen who could see into a person's soul was damned inconvenient. A few lies here and there weren't a big deal as far as Shay was concerned. They could help a person slide through life with less pain.

"When Brownstone dealt with the Harriken before," Shay began, "they apparently didn't learn their lesson. Instead of becoming afraid, they got even more pissed off."

"So much death and hurt, and they still aren't satisfied?" Alison looked down and shook her head. "It wasn't enough that they hurt my mom and got punished?"

"Some people just have thick skulls. The Harriken have placed a price on James' head; a big price, to get a lot of killers after him. Dumb killers, sure. After all, they *are* going after Brownstone. But these are still professional killers, and Brownstone is now lying low and trying to figure out a way to...*resolve* the problem."

Alison looked at Shay, her eyes unfocused as usual, but the weight of her gaze still as heavy as any sighted person's stare. "By 'resolving the problem' you mean he's going to...kill them all, right?"

Shay sighed. "Not necessarily. A lot of that is up to the men chasing him. You have to understand...Brownstone doesn't pick fights with people unless it involves bounties or personal stuff."

"What about me? I mean, there was no bounty on the Harriken when he helped me."

"You helped him find his dog, so it became personal. After that, well, it got even more personal."

Alison wiped a few tears from her eyes. "Do you think this is my fault?"

"No, Alison, not at all. Some bad guys did some sh—Stuff they shouldn't have and they got punished, and now more bad guys didn't learn their lesson. The Harriken had a lot of chances to walk away from all of this, even before Brownstone went and…uh, *resolved* some problems he had with them." Shay ran a hand through her hair. "Anyway, the point is that if some dumbass wants to come after him, that's on them. He's not gonna go out of his way to kill them, but he's not going to restrain himself either. That's just for the hired guns. The Harriken have made this way too personal, and I don't think he's gonna stop until they're eradicated."

Alison let out a quiet sigh. "From LA?"

Shay shook her head. "Don't be surprised if Brownstone decides to extend his reach a little."

The teen's lips pursed and a dark expression settled over her face.

"Are you okay?" Shay asked.

Alison nodded. "I'm just…tired of people hurting the people I love. I'll admit that I don't like feeling this way, but I'm experiencing an overwhelming urge to hurt people."

Shay sat down next to Alison and pulled her into an embrace. "Don't worry, Alison. We're gonna make sure you never have to."

## 16

Rays of sunlight broke through the darkened clouds as James continued trudging south through the hills and wet grasslands. He'd made good progress, and the clearing weather couldn't have happened at a better time.

*Maybe I'm luckier than you think, Professor. This plan will work, and it'll be fucking funny to see those bastards' faces when they realize what I've done, even if I hate this shit for being so complicated. Fucking Harriken.*

The sky had stopped pouring rain about an hour prior. James was thoroughly soaked and chilled, but more important than warming up was getting the attention of the authorities or the men tracking him. Either would work.

Like an iguana desperate for warmth, James found a tall outcropping and climbed it. When he got to the top he removed his hat. People needed to see his face for the next part of his plan to work.

*I knew I kept a flare gun in my go-case for some reason.*

The bounty hunter fished around in his backpack until he found the flare gun and shot a red flare into the sky. Then he settled in to munch on a rib.

Still good, even cold.

Several minutes passed, but nothing happened.

"Come on, guys. Don't do this to me. This is why I hate plans with a bunch of parts."

James loaded the gun again and sent off another flare. For good measure he repeated his actions thirty seconds later, leaving him with only a single flare.

*Maybe I'm too far south, or not south enough. Guess I'll hang onto the last one. Don't want to have to start a fire to get attention, even if it is wet. Not gonna burn down half of Southern California just to save my sorry ass.*

The bounty hunter replaced the flare gun in his pack and returned his attention to the ribs and a bottle of water.

After about five minutes, movement in the sky caught James' attention. He grinned and stood to wait. A dark form closed on him and the size and flashing red and blue lights identified it as a police drone even before he was able to see its shape in detail.

"Attention, citizen," a voice said from a speaker on the bottom of the drone. "This is the Rancho Santa Margarita Police Department. Your location has been noted, and we are preparing to dispatch a rescue team. Please remain where you are."

James waved at the drone and grabbed his phone to place a call to the Rancho Santa Margarita Police Department directly rather than 9-1-1. It was important that people see him, not just that he called his position in. The bait had to be strong and tasty to land the fish he wanted.

"Rancho Santa Margarita Police Department, how may I direct your call?" a chipper woman answered.

"Right now your people have a drone hovering above me in the hills southeast of Coto de Caza," James began. "I launched flares, but you don't need to send a rescue team. My name is James Brownstone, and I'm just going for a hike."

"Sir, I think—"

James hung up before she could get anything else out. He finished up a rib and tossed the bone on the ground.

Grinning, he stretched and hopped off the rock to continue hiking south.

*Game on, bitches.*

---

Larry liked his job as a security guard for Coto de Caza, even if a lot of the residents acted so arrogant. The pay was nice, and he didn't have to do much besides sit in the gatehouse all day. When some panicky trophy wife saw something in the bushes the police handled the situation; his involvement was limited to calling them. It was the easiest job he'd ever had, and on most days it wasn't stressful at all.

Mainly because he'd never had to stare down the barrel of a gun before.

Larry swallowed and kept his hands above his head. At least he hadn't wet himself. "Look, uh...you don't have to do this. I don't have any money in here...or anything worth stealing."

Two men with shaved heads and teardrop tattoos

below their eyes sat in a black Corvette. The passenger had a gun aimed at Larry.

"I have two simple questions for you, pal," the passenger said. "If you answer them right you get to live. If you answer them wrong you get to die. Understand?"

Larry gave a quick nod.

The man shook his head. "Say it."

"I understand, sir."

The gunman nodded and a grin appeared on his face as if he were savoring the fear. "First question: can you open the gate?"

"Uh, yes. Should I?" Larry kept his hands up, worried that a sudden move would end with him being shot.

"No, not yet. Second question: did some ugly fucker come through here earlier? He'd have like weird birthmarks on his face, tattoos, weird ridges, driving some shithole Humvee. James Brownstone?"

Larry frowned. "I knew that guy didn't belong here. Business meeting, my ass. But he said his name was Thomas McCartney, not James Brownstone."

The man with the gun grinned widely, revealing a bright gold tooth, and looked at the driver. "Check that shit out! Brownstone running around with a fake name. That means he's fucking scared, bro."

The driver gave a nod. "Little bitch."

The gunman looked back at Larry. "That answers my questions. Look, we've got no beef with anyone in your little fenced-off wonderland. We bag Brownstone, we make a lot more money than we could get from whatever bullshit you got here." He tapped the gun on the door. "We're here to do you a favor."

"A favor?"

"Yeah. A piece of garbage got through and we're the garbage collectors, so you're gonna let us through and we'll go take care of it. Understand? But if we hear any sirens, we're gonna come back here and start shooting. Understand?"

"I understand." Larry swallowed and nodded. He lowered his arm and pressed the button. The gate rumbled open, and he held his breath while he waited to see if he would survive.

"Little piece of advice there, pal," the man with the gun said. "I'd tell everyone in the community to stay inside for a while." He winked. "I'm a pro, though. I try not to kill anyone I don't get paid for. Not worth the cost of the bullets." He nodded at the driver. "Let's do this, bro."

The Corvette pulled through the gate and Larry let out a sigh of relief. His heart rate kicked up even more when another car pulled through behind the 'Vette, followed by a truck and a motorcycle.

Larry groaned. "I'm going to lose my job."

---

"Your boy certainly isn't keeping a low profile, Mack," Maria remarked, staring at the video the RSMPD had sent their way. "It's like he wants them to find him. He is *such* a cocky sonofabitch."

Sergeant Mack pulled out his phone and dialed Brownstone. He was certain the bounty hunter had a reason for what he was doing, but he wanted to make sure he hadn't just given up.

"Hey, Mack," Brownstone answered, voice as casual as ever. "This rain's been crazy."

"I've mostly been inside. Anyway, I'm not calling to chitchat."

"Then what are you calling for?"

"To ask you what the hell you are doing," Mack ground out through gritted teeth. "You were home free with that storm, and then you went out of your way to attract attention. You could have maybe hidden out until the heat died down."

"Yeah, I can understand how you'd see it that way."

"I've been busting my balls to get you some help and get these assholes off your back, but then you pulled that stunt with the flare. I just saw it on the computer. If the RSMPD is spreading that shit around, it means probably half the hitmen after you are now heading toward Coto de Caza."

Brownstone grunted. "That's the point."

"Brownstone, our drones have tagged at least five hitmen heading toward you. Are you saying that's what you wanted?"

Maria, Delroy, and Weber all looked at Mack with curiosity on their faces.

"I'm not near the rich people's houses," Brownstone assured him. "Come on, running away isn't gonna solve this. I've got to convince these assholes it's not worth following me, and to do that I need to do something real flashy." He grunted. "What are you worried about, anyway? I'm out in the wilderness, away from people. I've got a plan, but it works best if I get most of the assholes after me there together."

Mack snorted. "So you've got a plan? Care to share it with the rest of the class?"

"Nope. I trust you, Mack, but it's best you don't know what's going on. That way you'll all play the part I need."

"I hope you have a fucking clue what you're doing."

"Guess we'll find out soon enough. If not, thanks for being a good cop." Brownstone hung up.

"Did I hear you right?" Maria asked. "He *wanted* his position leaked?"

The sergeant sighed and nodded slowly. "Sounds like it. He's got some sort of plan to handle all the hitmen at once."

"Weber," the lieutenant ordered, "make sure you add trespassing to Brownstone's list of accomplishments. That's private land he's on right now."

Weber entered the note on the computer. "Recorded, Lieutenant."

Delroy chuckled. "Your boy sure likes to keep it flashy, but I've been thinking that even after the hitman shit is taken care of that still leaves us with a big issue."

"What issue?" Mack asked.

"The Harriken. I mean, Ikeda's in town, which means they're going to be a lot more aggressive in re-establishing themselves. We might miss the old Harriken after this is all done." Delroy furrowed his brow. "And the power vacuum could lead to serious clashes unless the Harriken are completely taken out."

Maria tried to take a sip of coffee, only to find that her cup was empty. "Weber, go get me some more coffee."

Weber grabbed her mug and headed out of the room.

The two other men chuckled and shook their heads.

"The Harriken can be handled like any other group of

normal criminals," Maria said. "I don't see what the big deal is. They might have started this problem, but the main issue at the moment is Brownstone."

Delroy nodded toward one of the screens displaying a frozen image of Brownstone. "I'm just saying that since we're already playing it fast and loose, maybe we should use this whole situation to clean house." He looked at Mack. "And that includes giving your boy what he wants."

"What do you mean?" Mack asked.

"Ikeda has been linked to the assassinations of federal agents, tons of cops, and at least one sitting congressman. The FBI said that attempting bombing of the Supreme Court last year had his fingerprints on it."

Mack shrugged. "He's a piece of cop-killing shit. Big surprise. What about it?"

The lieutenant scowled. "I see where you're going with this, Washington, and I don't like it. Not one fucking bit."

Mack looked at them. "I'm not following you."

"All those government and law enforcement targets, Mack," Delroy explained. "They change things, even if this guy isn't some big flashy asshole using magical artifacts. If we pushed just a little bit, we could get a dead-or-alive bounty issued on the entire organization all the way down, or at least on the local chapter because of what's going down. When Congress changed the law a few years back they put in some provisions that made it easier when dealing with organized crime, ever since that incident in Santa Fe." The detective nodded toward the screen with Brownstone's image. "The Harriken have given us what we need to take them down."

"So now you *want* Brownstone to do his thing, then?

Bloody damned vengeance?"

Weber entered the room with a fresh cup of coffee in hand. "Got your coffee, Lieutenant."

"That's bullshit," Maria thundered. "No fucking way." She stood and slashed her hand through the air.

"I'm pretty sure it's hazelnut," Weber told her, eyeing the cup with a confused look.

The lieutenant snatched cup from him and gestured with it at Delroy. "Not *you*, Weber. Washington's lost his mind."

Delroy chuckled. "I'm just saying the Harriken aren't going to last the weekend anyway, and I figure the least we can do is let Brownstone earn some cash. That way he can pay off all the fines his ass is generating. Plus, it sends a message to the Harriken and any other group that thinks they can do whatever the hell they want in our town."

"Another Brownstone fanboy? Perfect. I don't want to see him fined. I want to see him in a damned ultramax."

Delroy shrugged. "Let's just say maybe I think Mack had a point earlier, and I don't think taking Brownstone out of circulation is a good idea long-term. If this whole situation ends with a bunch more hitmen in jail and a lot of Harriken gone... Well, I don't know about you, but *I'm* going to sleep better at night."

Maria dropped into a chair, gazing at him with murderous intent. "Whatever. I'm going to keep adding to his list of infractions. I don't want Brownstone coming out ahead when this is all said and done." She focused her glare on Weber. "And when was this coffee made, Weber? The damned Ice Age? Go get me some coffee that is hotter than room temperature."

## 17

Too damn slow. *Damn*, are these guys slow. Geez, these fuckers are *SLOW*.

James watched the killers approach through his binoculars, wondering if he'd moved too far into the hills. Initially he'd spotted four vehicles, but in the end ten had shown up. Some of the trucks had tried to drive farther into the terrain, but the steep hills convinced everyone to give up on driving and hoof it sooner rather than later.

Once everyone unloaded from their vehicles, the bounty hunter determined he would be dealing with a total of twenty killers. They had spread out to make their individual ways through the hilly and rocky terrain in search of their payday.

James climbed the steep hill behind him. Once at the top, he pulled a small mirror from his backpack and held it up, letting the light reflect off it. The fish had gone for the bait, and now he needed to start reeling them in.

He dropped a second later. Bullets whizzed over him, accompanied by the crack of gunfire. If the enemy had been closer they might actually have stood a chance of hitting him, and he suspected that only the fact that such a large group of people were blasting away at him had resulted in any of the shots coming close.

A buzzing and glowing green bolt zoomed past where he'd been standing and continued into the distance, so at least one of them had ranged magic available.

At least he wasn't shooting that green shit through holes in the sky like that last douchebag.

James hurried down the opposite side of the hill from the hitmen. Now that they'd laid eyes on him they weren't going to give up.

He chuckled as he thought about the fact that the killers had naturally spread themselves out as they searched; no one had thought to take a few of the competition out. No honor among thieves, but plenty among professional killers, apparently.

*All you fuckers are suddenly singing Kumbaya and cooperating. I doubt you're all from the same organization, so how are you going to decide who gets the reward? Or are you just going to kill each other at the end for my head? I guess everyone else wins either way.*

The darkening sky threatened the return of the rain. James didn't mind. Most scenarios where the enemy couldn't shoot at him from long range worked to his advantage, especially since Mr. Green Buzzing Bolt was in the mix.

James arrived at the bottom of the hill and spotted another rockier hill a few hundred yards farther away. He picked up the pace, not wanting to get caught out in the open.

*Now how many of the bastards should I pick off? Too many will send them scurrying, and not enough might cause me trouble later. Plus, I need to leave enough of them to make sure everyone else hears about what went down.*

Fuck. Should have called Tyler and issued an invitation or some shit.

James grunted. Everything would be over soon if he kept moving south.

---

A couple more hours of hiking south through the increasingly rocky and hilly terrain in the rain were punctuated by rest periods where James waited for the idiots to catch up. The intermittent rain helped keep him from being picked off from a distance, but also meant the pack after him kept losing him. He'd had to arrange a mistakenly kicked rock or errant flash of light to reveal his location more than once.

*Yeah, that's your problem. You guys are thinking too city. Should have anticipated my path and set up a sniper or something. Maybe you'd have had a chance.*

James patted a pouch containing his potions. Assuming no one killed him he could survive a lot of damage—even without the amulet—with the help of his healing potions, but he suspected he might need them for his showdown with the Harriken.

After a quick survey of the surrounding terrain, the bounty hunter decided to wait in a crag. He couldn't risk the hitmen getting tired and giving up, and he needed to give everyone a shot of adrenaline by introducing himself up close and personal to some of the killers.

*Maybe I should have just waited at the ruins of my house and told people to stop by. I could have spent a week killing every asshole who came up. They wouldn't all have had rocket launchers.*

Since no one had picked him off with a high-powered rifle yet, James assumed his pursuers were mostly a pistol-and-shotgun crew. Mr. Green Buzzing Bolt seemed to have good range, but poor aim. He suspected the man was used to tossing his magic around at much closer range.

The twenty hitmen now walked in three groups about fifty yards apart. The frontrunners, three men in gray urban camouflage fatigues who were armed with pistols, made their way carefully toward the last position they'd spotted him in. From what he'd seen earlier they weren't Grayson, so he assumed they were from a different company.

*Of course, you're wearing urban camouflage in the middle of the wilderness. You're not exactly blending into the terrain here, assholes.*

James also doubted that Grayson would be dumb enough to come after him with only three guys, given that they believed he'd slaughtered an entire unit. It didn't matter if it wasn't true. It only mattered that they believed it.

*Maybe if I write them a nice letter explaining that I didn't kill their guys they'll lay off. Then again, the assholes were planning to ambush and kill me before, so yeah, fuck them. I'll take out the Harriken, then maybe Grayson will get the damned point.*

James glanced down at the slight bump in his shirt marking his amulet. The whole point of the plan was to avoid having to use his amulet. He hadn't had to use it yet, but he hadn't had to deal with such a large group until now—and at least one man had access to magic.

Time to make this chase a little more exciting.

The bounty hunter surveyed the area, and a smile came to his face as he spotted a good hiding place—a ledge with thick sides that jutted out from the rocky hill. He scurried up the rocks and flattened himself to wait.

*Always wanted to try this out even if it seems a little chickenshit.*

James pulled out a knife and waited still as a statue as the crunch of boots on rocks joined the slight howl of the wind. The whole ninja-lying-in-wait strategy wasn't really his style, but just bolting out and killing everyone would ruin his plan.

"I know I saw him around here," one of the mercenaries said in a low voice as they got closer. "Must have already crossed over to the other side of this damn hill. That fucker can move fast."

Another man laughed. "You know, I heard all this shit about how tough Brownstone is, but in the end he ran off to hide like a little bitch. The Harriken aren't so tough if they are afraid of this guy."

"Hey, according to what I just read, the little bitch is now worth six hundred thousand," the third man chimed in. "I don't care if the Harriken are weak-ass bitches. I just care about their money."

*Six hundred thousand? Man, if I'd known they were going to keep increasing the bounty I might have gone for a few more days and gotten it up to a million, just so I could brag about it.*

The scrape and thud of the boots against rock grew closer until it was right below James. He waited, his breath held, for all three men to pass under him.

James didn't yell, scream, or offer any pithy one-liners. Instead, he rolled off the side of the ledge and landed right behind the first mercenary, then reached around and slit his throat. The gurgling mercenary managed to squeeze off a single round into the air.

The bounty hunter held the man up, not letting him fall to the ground. The other two mercenaries spun, raising their guns, and James sent a throwing knife into the head of the first. He shoved the dying mercenary toward the second and lunged toward the man.

The merc squeezed off several rounds and the body Brownstone had propelled toward him jerked as it took the hits. The distraction gave James enough time to close on him. He grabbed the man's gun and thrust it upward before slamming his fist into the man's stomach.

James yanked on the pistol as the mercenary flew backward several yards, landing hard on the rocky terrain and rolling. The man gasped for breath and coughed up blood. A second later Brownstone shot him in the head with his own pistol.

Bullets pelted the rocks and dirt around him. He tossed the pistol to the ground and hurriedly pulled his knife out of the second mercenary's throat. A green bolt exploded into the ledge above him, showering him with shards of rock.

James sprinted away from the three dead mercenaries and the remaining killers.

*Mission accomplished. That should be enough to keep them after me.*

---

Colonel Grayson was behind his desk in his office, thumbing through manila folders containing personnel files for new recruits. He didn't care if it would be more efficient to do it on the computer. Something about the old-fashioned approach always seemed more effective to him, as if handling the actual files somehow gave him better insight into the men who might want to join his company.

The Brownstone matter would be resolved soon enough, one way or another, and it was important that he focus on rebuilding the strength and reputation of Grayson PMC Services.

"You've caused me quite a lot of trouble, Mr. Brownstone," the colonel muttered. "It'd be helpful to me if you would die soon."

Someone knocked sharply on the door.

"Come in."

The door swung open to reveal Major Tallmadge, who strode in and saluted Grayson. The colonel saluted back.

"What is it, Major?"

"I just got some intel that might give us additional leverage in the Brownstone matter."

The colonel folded his hands in front of him. "Leverage?"

"Yes."

Colonel Grayson didn't like the self-satisfied grin on the major's face, but he did like what he was hearing. Strength was almost an afterthought when it came to winning a conflict; proper intelligence and logistics were the true keys. If they'd had better intelligence on Brownstone they wouldn't have suffered the losses they had.

"Elaborate, Major," the colonel ordered.

"There's a girl—a teenager—who has a connection to Brownstone. We're not sure if she's a relative or just a friend or something, but she's going to a school on the East Coast. Some sort of government place for training people with magic. It might not be a good idea to go after her there, but maybe when she comes home we could capture her."

The colonel snorted. "A school is a school. It's a place filled with soft trainers and children. It's like suggesting a bunch of kids at a military prep school would present any risk to real soldiers." He shook his head. "No, I don't care if they can do some magic tricks. A bullet to the brain will stop that quickly enough. Find out more about her. We might just have to send someone to pay her a visit."

---

The huge bear of a drunk, whom Tyler had learned was named Ben, eyed him suspiciously.

For all the profit the bartender was making, he was realizing how annoying it was when there were so many people in the bar.

"What?" Tyler challenged. "You have a problem?"

Ben shrugged. "Maybe. Did I just hear you place a big side bet that said Brownstone won't even be killed? That's not even one of the fucking options on your board." He pointed to the chalkboard. "And, what…you think Brownstone's gonna live now?"

Tyler ground his teeth. The stupid drunks were more perceptive than he had realized.

"Yes, I placed the bet. What do *you* fucking care?"

"You're fucking supporting Brownstone with your money, idiot. I thought you hated Brownstone."

Several nearby patrons turned to stare at Tyler with a mix of anger and confusion on their faces.

"I'm not supporting Brownstone," Tyler announced, raising his voice so everyone could hear. "I'm hedging my happiness."

Ben narrowed his bloodshot eyes. "What the fuck does that mean?"

Tyler sneered at the man, then pushed through the crowd to the chalkboard. "It's like hedging your bet on roulette: when you put some money down on black even though you think red is going to hit." He waved at the board. "If Brownstone dies I'm a happy man, but if he gets his ass out of this predicament…" He shrugged. "Well, at least I'll have more money in my pocket."

# 18

Shay sat across from Alison at a table in the dining hall, nibbling on some moist chicken. Or at least she thought it was chicken. It smelled like chicken and tasted like chicken, but she couldn't ignore that she was at a magic school.

She eyed the breast on her plate. No strange patterns, no glow.

"This isn't some weird Oriceran bird, is it? I mean, it *tastes* like chicken, but maybe that's just some spell."

Alison laughed. "No one would waste magic just to make something taste like chicken."

"Huh. Maybe. Ever wonder why so many things taste like chicken, though? Maybe there *is* a spell after all." Shay shrugged.

"It's just baked chicken, Aunt Shay. No magic." The teen winked. "I promise."

Shay took another bite. Moist and well-seasoned; nice food for a school. She swallowed and then cleared her throat. "I read the other day about how some environmentalist groups want MMO warning labels added to anything magic has touched. They were mad about some companies using magic to help grow crops, especially in certain places with crappy soil."

Alison blinked. "MMO?"

"Magically-modified organism. A lot of people have been going on about the potential health risks and all that, saying a lot of us might end up with cancer in thirty years because of traces of magic in food and water. There's even going to be a vote on a referendum about it in California in the next election. If it passes, people will have to label any food that comes in contact with magic at any point from when it's grown or caught to when it gets to the store, even if it's just like there was a witch nearby casting spells when they packed it."

The teen rolled her eyes. "The Oricerans have been dealing with magic since before humans had any real civilizations. I think they know what's dangerous and what's not."

"Maybe." Shay shrugged.

Alison sighed. "You don't agree?"

"I hadn't thought about it much, but the last thing I expect to die from is magical cancer." Shay smiled. "Hey, don't get too worked up, kid. That's just California for you. Obviously Virginia is a little looser about that stuff considering they have a magic school here, but back in California I still have to read a notice about how my coffee might give me cancer every time I pick some up from a Starbucks." Shay winked. "Got all offended on behalf of Oriceran, eh? Going native just because you're learning magic?"

Alison's cheeks reddened. "No, it's not that. I've learned a lot since coming here, and I'm just, you know, *frustrated*."

Shay looked at the young woman. "Why? Because of the whole delayed-magic-potential thing?"

Alison shook her head. "No, not that at all. It's because we've been taught so many things that aren't true. The problem is that our historians are wrong, lying, or both. I've been studying a lot about the true history of our world since coming here. Of both worlds."

Shay nodded slowly. "Yeah, in my own research I've learned that a lot of the sh— Stuff I grew up believing isn't true. At least you grew up knowing that magic is a real thing. What sort of things have they taught you here?"

"A lot of the gods in the ancient religions weren't just metaphors for royalty or made-up stories, but people with magic or even Oricerans. How do you think the Great Pyramids got built? Just a bunch of guys moving stones with these really exact measurements?"

Shay laughed and raised her hands. "You don't have to convince me. I've been to them. I know how much of what we think about our ancient history isn't true, and how true a lot of reports we dismissed as stories actually *are* true. It's still weird trying to wrap your mind around it. It's like the world in general is shrugging about it, but that doesn't mean it's any less true."

Alison nodded. "I read about how there are all these little statues they found in Japan from over ten thousand years ago. They look like little astronauts and some people thought they were modeled after alien astronauts, but they actually represent Oricerans who came over there wearing magic armor to help some of the people in that area."

Alison frowned. "I've also been taught that a lot of the age estimates for ancient artifacts are way off. Magic can mess up a lot of the archaeology techniques like carbon dating, so there are a lot of ruins and stuff out there that are actually way older than people know."

Shay chuckled. "I've read about that. There's been some pushback in the archaeology communities, both freelance and the more academic. Don't know that I care all that much since I'm more concerned about magical artifacts than history, but I believe the dating's often wrong." She shrugged. "It's hard to argue with magic. I believe in it, and as far I'm concerned all this is great for my profession."

"What do you mean?"

"Just as an example, before, no one knew if Atlantis was real. Now we know it was, and it was advanced because of Oriceran magic. There are all sorts of lost cities and ancient ruins linked to Oriceran, so it means there are a lot more opportunities to find treasure...I mean, uh, *things of interest*, now that magic's growing stronger on Earth. Plus, there are things that were hidden by magic that we didn't even know to look for before."

Alison looked away from Shay, staring around the dining hall at the students chatting with one another.

"I guess the other thing that I find frustrating is that a lot of people keep acting like Oricerans don't belong on Earth."

Shay picked up her glass of water to take a sip. "People will always find a reason to not like someone different. That's kind of what defines humanity."

Alison reached for her own drink. "I know, but Earth and Oriceran have such a long history together. It's kind of strange for people to act like Oriceran is new when they've touched so many places and civilizations throughout our history. Why can't everyone just get along?"

A dark chuckle escaped Shay's mouth. "It'll take a lot more than magic to get that to happen."

---

Gordon stepped around the rock, using it to keep himself upright on the steep slope. He wiped off some of the sweat beading on his shaved head and glanced at his brother. Sweat covered the other man's reddened face.

"You doing okay, Darrell?"

His brother nodded. "Fine. Just want to end Brownstone already. How fucking long have we been chasing him? I want to catch up to that motherfucker."

The waning sun signaled the coming turnover between day and night. Gordon gritted his teeth. Losing Brownstone in the middle of the fucking hills at night meant they'd probably lose him forever. The bastard would keep running south, and the next thing they heard it'd probably be some Mexican hitman taking him down.

"Just think about how much money we're gonna collect, bro," Gordon reminded Darrell, glancing over his shoulder at the loose formation of hitmen trailing them.

After Brownstone had killed the three mercs, Gordon hoped he would thin out the herd a little more. Eventually things were going to get sticky about who would get to keep Brownstone's head, and Gordon didn't want to have to take on more than a dozen men over the bounty.

Instead, the damned bounty hunter kept running.

*Fucking pussy. You can't run from us forever.*

"I see something, bro," Darrell shouted, and pointed.

Gordon snapped his head in that direction. Something glinted in the distance.

"Fucking idiot. We wouldn't even be able to follow him if he wouldn't keep messing up like that. Fucker's too used to being the one chasing."

The hitman ran toward the glint. His brother followed, and soon the entire little army was sprinting at top speed, their breathing ragged and labored as they attempted to close on their target.

A good half-mile later Gordon slowed, looking around and kicking the dirt. "Where the fuck did he go? It was like he was here, then just disappeared."

Darrell gestured to the south. "There are some bushes and rocks and shit over there. He was running that way. Let's just keep going that way."

The gathered hitmen had made it another three hundred yards when Gordon spotted movement from the corner of his eye.

The hitman spun, raising his gun. "Time to die, Brownstone."

The ground suddenly birthed strange humanoid plants, or at least that was what it looked like at first. It took Gordon's brain a few seconds to realize he wasn't surrounded by magical monstrosities, but dozens upon dozens of men in ghillie suits—maybe even a hundred—pointing assault rifles at his group.

The hitman spun, seeking an escape route, but the ghillie-suited men surrounded the hitmen on all sides. The killers all raised their guns and exchanged nervous glances.

"United States Marine Corps!" shouted one of the ghillie-suited men. "Drop your weapons or we will drop *you!*"

Gordon jerked his head around, his heart thundering. It wasn't fucking fair. They were supposed to have the advantage. They were hunting Brownstone as a pack, but there was no way they were going to win against a whole unit of Marines.

"Drop your weapons, go to your knees, and put your hands on your heads," shouted the Marine who had spoken before. "You have thirty seconds, or we will light you up."

Gordon let his pistol fall to the ground along with his knees, and he laced his hands behind his head. "Fucking, Brownstone," he muttered under his breath. "How did you pull this shit off?"

The rest of the pack complied, all except for one. He threw his hand out and a magical green bolt shot toward a Marine. Another Marine pushed the target out of the way and the bolt buzzed over their heads, exploding into the ground a few seconds later.

Gordon had never before seen a man hit by bullets from dozens of assault rifles simultaneously. One second he was there, the next he had exploded in a shower of blood.

"Cease fire! Cease fire!"

The Marines surged forward to secure the surviving prisoners with zip-ties.

The Marine who had shouted the commands earlier stomped up to Gordon, who was the closest of any of the hitmen. "What kind of fucking morons do you have to be that you would show up heavily armed and invade Camp

Pendleton?" He leaned forward. "It was a useful training exercise for us, though. Got to give you that."

Gordon glared at the Marine, resisting the urge to threaten the man who was obviously in charge.

The Marine grinned at him. "You know, I'm sure they're going to slap all sorts of terrorism charges on you assholes. Going to throw away the key, I bet. You better hope you don't have any bounties or warrants or you'll never see daylight again."

Another Marine laughed. "I sure as hell hope they *do* have bounties, Gunny. Since we caught them on base we can get the bounty, and that's some major fucking beer money."

The older Marine laughed and looked Gordon up and down. "Yeah. Good training exercise, and now beer money. Great day. *Really* great day!"

The gunnery sergeant looked up as Brownstone made his way through the Marines. Some of them eyed him with respect as he passed, and others with suspicion.

"Thanks for the help, Gunny," Brownstone said, extending his hand. The Marine gave it a firm shake.

Gordon glared at the bounty hunter, but the man ignored him.

"Don't worry about it, Brownstone," the gunnery sergeant told him. "It's nice when we can train the men in a more realistic scenario." He nodded toward the bloodied remains of the slain hitman. "Too bad he was stupid. It didn't have to go down like that."

Brownstone shrugged. "I hate to ask this of you, Gunny, but I've got one more favor."

The Marine chuckled. "What?"

"I need someone to give me a ride to a rental place. I need to rent another Humvee."

---

Esteban peered through Isabella's scope, leading Brownstone as the man walked through the crowd of Marines.

The hitman almost didn't believe what he'd witnessed. Brownstone was there one second, then he'd vanished. By the time he reappeared the Marines had surrounded the rest of the hitmen. Some of the top killing talent in Los Angeles would now be going to prison.

But not Esteban.

His patience had been rewarded, and his inferiors had been captured or killed. He couldn't kill Brownstone with the damned military men so close, but now that his prey thought he'd escaped the pack he would let his guard down —and Esteban would kill him and take his head.

"Tonight your head is mine."

"Nice rifle," a young woman remarked from behind Esteban. "Wonder what kind of range you get on that."

"I've made kills as far…" Esteban rolled, his hand going for the pistol in his shoulder holster.

He cried out as a 5.56×45mm bullet tore through this shoulder. His pistol dropped to the ground.

A young Marine MP lance corporal stood over him, her rifle pointed directly at him. Her nametape indicated that her last name was Vasquez. The fresh-faced enlisted didn't look like she was even in her twenties yet.

Vasquez kept her rifle trained on him, anger in her eyes.

"You know one of the first things they teach about shooting in boot camp?"

Esteban kept still, even though his shoulder throbbed. "What?"

"Don't shoot at anyone you're not willing to kill. You're lucky you only got shot in the shoulder." Vasquez gestured with her rifle. "Roll the fuck back over. And welcome to Camp Pendleton, you terrorist asshole."

Esteban rolled over with a grunt. He started to chuckle and it escalated into a loud laugh.

"What's so funny, asshole?" Vasquez hissed. "Don't give me another reason to shoot your ass."

"I was going to kill the ultimate prey when none other could. Yet you, some *puta* soldier girl, have defeated me." The hitman cackled. "Well played, Fate. Well played."

"Shut your mouth. And I'm no soldier, I'm a damned *Marine*."

# 19

James decided that if he were to ever replace the F-350, he might consider a Humvee. He'd just experienced the world's most expensive test drive, and he was impressed, even if he had now moved on to a second one. Contacting the original rental company about the first could wait a few days.

He stifled a yawn as he turned down the street toward the Leanan Sídhe. It'd been an exhausting couple of days, but he'd managed to drive all the way back to Los Angeles with nothing more than the occasional police drone following him. The current situation offered hope that he wouldn't be sucking on a rocket or fireball anytime soon.

The dark clouds lingered in the night sky and blocked the moon and the stars but the worst of the storm had passed, leaving only an occasional light shower.

James pulled into the lot behind the Irish pub and parked. When he stepped out of the truck, he did a cautious check of the area. Even though he assumed that most of the hitmen willing to go after him had been taken care of, it didn't hurt to be careful.

The bounty hunter made his way into the crowded bar. It didn't matter that it was late at night; the place was still packed, as always.

A comfortable familiarity settled over James and he smiled to himself as he navigated through the crowd toward the back, where the Professor sat drinking a beer. The older man's red face suggested it wasn't his first.

It was good to be back. All this complicated-plan shit was wearing him down. Fucking Harriken.

Most of the crowd parted for James, though several stared at him. He chuckled. His days of running, climbing, and a little bit of violence had left him looking as shabby as his coat.

He glanced down. It bore tears, dirt, and more than a few blood stains.

"Sorry, it's been a rough day," James rumbled when he got to the table and took a seat. He heaved a great sigh. "This shit is annoying."

The Professor laughed. "Aye, I'm sure it is, but you should know, lad, that word has gotten out, along with a few curious rumors."

"Like what?"

"They mention that you've killed several of the men after you, and now you seemingly have the Marine Corps on call." The Professor chuckled. "I suppose that's not even much of a rumor since it's been all over the news that a group of armed criminals attempted to invade Camp Pendleton and one was killed. According to the reporters, the group had become convinced that one James Brownstone was in the area. The Marines Corps are just saying the invaders should be treated as terrorists. No one's exactly weeping about the Marines gunning down a known hitman." He picked up his beer and swallowed a huge slug of it, then put a hand over his mouth and belched. "From what I understand, all the local freelancers have decided your hit contract is more trouble than it's worth. The Marine stunt fed into the narrative that the authorities are pulling out all the stops to help you, and that seems partially true from what I can tell."

"Good, my plan worked then. Dead bad guys, no dead innocent people, and the only property damage is my place." James shrugged. "Well, and one sad rental Humvee." He reached into his pocket and pulled out two rings, one polished onyx and the other a gold band with silver inlays. He slid them over to the Professor.

Smite-Williams slipped the rings into a jacket pocket with a smile. "Since you're not dead and the Marines caught all your new fans, it seems like these worked well for you. I'll be the first to admit that I didn't think your plan was all that great, but you pulled it off."

"Yep, worked perfectly. Slipped on the invisibility ring and then the floating one to pass right over the bastards." James chuckled. "You should have seen their faces when those Marines popped up. I could see the 'Oh, fuck, what the hell just happened?' in their eyes. That shit was funny as hell."

The Professor nodded slowly, smiling wryly. He picked up his beer and took a sip.

"Something wrong, Professor?"

"No, just... It's rare that you manage to surprise me. I

know a lot about you, lad, and I didn't know that you had enough clout with the Marines Corps to get them to help you on this. It's not like the military ever supports a bounty hunter who asks for help. I don't think even *I* could have pulled that off on such short notice."

James grinned. "What can I say? I'm a people person."

The older man laughed at that. "I know many people who might disagree with that statement."

"Yeah, okay, so I'm also a big asshole. Anyway, the truth is that anytime I'm in a bar I buy guys in uniform a beer if I can. You know, to show my respect, just like the donuts with the cops. I've been through San Diego a lot in the last couple of years. I ran into a Marine gunny there last winter and we hit it off, and he introduced me to some other people. He'd heard of me, and liked that I had taken down a few righteous assholes."

The Professor finished his beer and lowered his glass to the table. "It still strikes me as insanity that they agreed to your plan, but I'm glad it worked out. What now, then?"

"Tonight I'm planning on getting a good night's rest and a decent shower in a hotel. Tomorrow morning, I'm chowing down on some hot barbeque, and then I'll head to my house to see if anything survived the explosions and fire."

The Professor's smile faltered for a second. "It's not over, you know, even if you've frightened off the freelancers. The Harriken just used them to soften you up. They've brought in reinforcements."

James grunted. "I give exactly zero fucks. I figure I've bought enough time to relax for the night, but it doesn't matter. This ends sooner rather than later. I know where to go and what I need to do. I just had to make sure I didn't need to watch my back when I kicked in their front door."

"I almost feel sorry for the Harriken."

James snorted. "You should. They're all about to die."

---

After a night at a hotel, again under the name Thomas McCartney, James hit Phillips again to buy more ribs and offer the owner twice the cost of the Igloo by way of apology. His conscience taken care of, he headed toward where everything had all started: the blasted remains of his house.

His stomach knotted as he turned down his street. He wasn't worried about anyone attacking him there. If they were dumb enough to come after him he'd kill them, but facing the destruction of what little permanence he'd had in life was going to be difficult.

Ashes to ashes, dust to dust—especially when a rocket launcher was involved.

He sighed. *It wasn't that long ago that I had a simple life, a nice house, and a loyal dog. Now my dog's dead. My house is gone, and I don't even have my signed recipe books anymore.*

*It didn't have to go down this way. All I wanted to do was help out a girl who helped me find my dog, but you fuckers had to push me back.*

*All you had to do was not kill Leeroy.*

James parked the Humvee on the street and hopped out. He stared at the rental vehicle for a moment and rubbed his chin.

When he went after the Harriken he'd make sure to

keep this truck way back. Didn't want to have to pay for *two* Humvees.

The bounty hunter's eyes narrowed as he surveyed the remains of his house. While the destruction had been near total, the wood fragments had been gathered into several neatly stacked piles. The yard and driveway were both free of debris, and even the scorched sidewalk in front had been swept clean.

James stepped toward what had once been his home. The top levels were more of a bare outline than a structure, and the darkened and scorched remains of half his house provided evidence of the destruction from the secondary explosion.

There was no separation anymore between the basement and the ground floor. The explosions, or perhaps whoever had cleaned up, had removed the few remaining parts of the basement ceiling. What was left resembled a partially-excavated ash-filled pit more than anything else.

Nothing remained of the stairs, but James spotted several ladders. The bounty hunter narrowed his eyes as he looked around. Melted metal and burned wood still lay in the ashes, but he didn't spot any of the fireproof strongboxes or safes that had held valuables and equipment.

"Fuck," James muttered. "Of course some fuckers looted my place. Probably those Harriken bastards, to *really* make a point. Well, I'm gonna make my own point, assholes."

He shook his head and turned back toward the Humvee. At least the looters had cleaned everything else up. He didn't know if he would keep the land. It'd make more sense to buy a new house…and maybe it was time to leave the neighborhood. He wasn't sure.

"I'll cut you a break, you looter assholes," the bounty hunter muttered. "I won't track your asses down and kill every last one of you until I've finished off the Harriken, assuming you aren't them. That should give you enough time to run away. Enjoy my shit."

The roar of an engine and the heavy thump of bass reached his ears as a red Ford pickup took a hard turn around the corner and sped toward James.

"I tried to give you a break," James growled. "But you just have to keep pushing and pushing and fucking pushing."

James gritted his teeth and yanked out a .45. The truck closed, and he grunted, ready to lay out anyone who was still stupid enough at this point to attack him.

Anger coursed through him as he saw the kind of truck they were driving.

*Those fuckers have the balls to come after me in an F-350? I will fucking end them!*

The F-350 screeched to a halt and James raised his gun, and the tinted window rolled down to reveal not an assassin but Trey with his hands up.

"Woah," the gang leader exclaimed. "Don't shoot just because you're jealous of my sweet-ass new ride, motherfucker. That's some petty-ass bullshit, Mr. Brownstone."

James snorted and holstered his weapon. "Since when do you drive a truck, let alone an old truck like this, Trey?"

The bounty hunter shook his head. He had to admit that it was in fact a sweet-ass ride.

Trey stepped out of the vehicle. "I've been looking for one for a while. I've always been jealous of yours." The gang leader slammed the door and shook his head as he surveyed the property. "We tried to clean up here best we could. Only so much we could do, though. Sorry, motherfucker."

James looked over his shoulder. "That explains some of this, then."

The gang leader looked down, frowning "We fucking let you down, Mr. Brownstone. We let those bitches roll right up and blow your motherfucking house up like it weren't nothing. That's a bitch-slap against you and a bitch-slap against me and my boys." He looked up, his expression fierce. "If you know who they are and they still breathin', you just point and me and my boys will roll over there and fuck 'em up. We'll make 'em sorry they ever dared fuck with our hood and the mighty motherfucking Mr. James Brownstone."

James pursed his lips, eyeing the gang leader. "I don't know the exact people who did it, but it doesn't matter. The Harriken started it, so I'm going to just go have a loud, violent, and one-way discussion with them, now that I've handled some of the other people."

"I heard you got them shot up by motherfucking Marines. Like you Chesty Puller and shit."

"They only killed one guy. I killed more than that over the last couple of days."

Trey laughed. "Never doubted it. Stupid motherfuckers shouldn'ta come after you."

"As for everything else, it wasn't your fault. It was a fast and professional hit." James stared at the ruins of his house. "Even I was surprised. Do you know why I'm not dead?"

Trey pumped a fist in the air. "Because you're motherfucking James Brownstone and you could kick the Devil's ass. One of my boys saw you storm out of the burning house like it weren't no thing."

He shook his head. "I'm still alive because I was in the basement when they attacked, Trey. If I'd been upstairs I'd have been dead." He locked eyes with the gang leader. "Keep that in mind. I'm not gonna lie and pretend I can't and haven't beat down a lot of tough assholes, but the truth is, sometimes it's just about luck. Right place. Right time. You could be the toughest fucker in the world, but then you turn your back and someone sneaks up on you."

"My nana always says we make our luck, and she's fucking ninety-two and could still beat down half my boys with her cane. I figure she's on to something."

"Probably." James looked over his shoulder at the ruins. "I do have a favor to ask."

"Whatever you ask, Mr. Brownstone, me and my boys will deliver. Even if you say it ain't our fault, it's the least we can do for letting these fuckers diss you like that. That offer is up to and including wasting their motherfucking asses."

"I don't need you to kill anyone. I know not everything will have survived, but I had some lockboxes and safes that held valuables and some equipment in the basement. It looks like someone looted it. I need you to ask around. I don't need the guys dead. If they're willing to give it back, I'll let it go for now."

A huge grin split Trey's face, and he walked to the back of the truck and slapped the side. "Look inside, motherfucker. That's why I'm here. When one of my boys called and said he saw you in the hood, I decided it was time for me to become motherfucking UPS."

James stepped over to look into the truck bed. Scorched lockboxes and safes filled the back.

"I wanted to make sure no bitches jacked your shit while you were off handling your business," Trey told him, his arms crossed and a smug smile on his face. "I did have to beat down one of my boys for trying to steal from you. I ain't killed him or nothing, but he learned his lesson about respect and not being a whiny-ass bitch."

James picked up a strongbox and then set it down on the sidewalk.

Trey's eyebrows lifted. "Not that I'd be all objecting if you wanted to donate your treasure to me and my boys, but you don't need that shit. Ain't that why you asked?"

"Since you already found my stuff, I have another favor to ask."

"What?"

"Hold onto it for a couple more days." James patted one of the containers. "I'll pay you a finder's and storage fee. I still have some ass to kick, and I don't want this shit getting blown up during that."

Trey gave James a little salute. "I like the sound of a finder's fee."

James headed toward the Humvee. "Your grandmother's partially right, you know."

"About the luck shit?"

"Yeah. We *do* make our own luck." The bounty hunter gave Trey a feral grin. "But we can also make other people's luck."

"No shit?"

James nodded. "Yeah, and the Harriken's luck just ran out."

# 20

Between the end of the hitman hunt and Trey's gang returning all of his strongboxes and safes, James allowed a bit of satisfaction to settle in.

The enemy's forces had been weakened, and it was time to go straight for the enemy stronghold and finish off the bastards who seemed incapable of learning their damned lesson.

*It's pretty damned simple, assholes: don't fuck with me and you'll continue breathing.*

The bounty hunter pulled into a parking lot next to a shady-looking laundromat. It'd been a while since he checked his messages, and he needed to make sure he could launch the final assault with no other concerns.

A message from Shay informed him that Alison was still doing okay and there were no signs of anyone coming after her.

James nodded to himself. *I'm glad Shay decided to go to Virginia. This shit would have been hard if I had to worry about*

*Alison. Definitely have to take Shay to her fancy restaurant after this is all over.*

Most of his other messages related to barbeque podcasts and barbeque-site updates, but one FROM line with an unusual source caught his eye: Sergeant Jackson Mack, LAPD.

James opened the email and frowned, confused by its brevity.

**Check out the recent bounties, Brownstone.**

The bounty hunter stared at the message, wondering if Mack had forgotten to send the rest. The cop had to know that James still needed to deal with the Harriken and didn't have time to go after any bounties, even major ones. Maybe it was proof of his faith in the bounty hunter's ability to finish off the gangsters and live.

James pulled up the LAPD Bounty Hunter Outreach Department app and looked in the 'Hot New Bounties' Section just to be sure he wasn't missing out on something obvious—and that King Pyro or Sombra hadn't returned from the dead. He wouldn't put it past the latter.

What the hell?

The bounty hunter reread the latest bounty notice three times to make sure he understood what he was seeing. The government had issued a dead-or-alive organizational bounty on the Harriken in LA.

In the United States, James had mostly seen organizational bounties applied to terrorist groups. From what he could tell from the notice any Harriken who surrendered to the police immediately would be exempt, but otherwise it was open season on the Japanese gangsters if a bounty hunter was brave enough—or dumb enough—to go after an entire vicious gang.

*Too bad they couldn't have fucking done this before when I laid out tons of those guys. How much money would I have earned?*

James allowed a grin to appear on his face. Now he understood why the Professor had been so surprised.

The cops had turned the tables on the Harriken.

Even if people didn't want to go after the whole organization, individual Harriken on the street could be taken down by other bounty hunters. It wasn't like a person needed to be a Class-Six bounty hunter to take on an individual Harriken enforcer. From what James had seen they relied on swords and guns, not magic.

But James didn't want the gangsters to suffer a death by a thousand cuts. He wanted to smash their fucking faces in and make them pay for the destruction of his home and possessions. Most importantly, the bounty hunter wanted the Harriken to know that James Brownstone was the man delivering their pain.

"Some of those pit-masters who signed those books aren't even alive anymore, fuckers," James rumbled.

The level of intervention necessary to get an organizational bounty, even one limited to the city level, exceeded the power of someone like Sergeant Mack. Some high-ranking people in the LAPD would have had to push for this type of bounty to be issued, which meant several people had tried to intervene on his behalf, likely from multiple departments.

*I thought half the LAPD hated my ass?* He shrugged. Maybe they liked him more than he knew.

It occurred to James that someone in the LAPD might have seen the opportunity for him to clean house for them. If he died it was as a bounty hunter going after bounties, but if he succeeded he could cripple the Harriken and put an end to their attempt to reestablish themselves in Los Angeles.

In the end it didn't matter. He was going after the Harriken anyway, and at least now he'd get paid for it. Even with his savings, valuables, and investments, he'd lost a house, needed to fix his truck, and had to pay for a damaged Humvee.

That shit added up.

James closed the app and went back to looking through his email. An odd subject line caught his eye: WHEN YOU ABSOLUTELY *MUST* KILL JAPANESE SWORDSMEN. The return address was the customer service department at a hospital with no name. A note at the top read, "We share a very attractive mutual friend."

Who the fuck were they even talking about? The Professor?

The bounty hunter grunted and scanned the rest of the mail. The body of the message included several maps detailing the layout of the building the Harriken were using as their temporary headquarters, along with information on their likely defenses including drones and sniper placement. It'd be a much tougher fight than when he'd raided them the last time, and he didn't have Shay backing him up for this one.

James grunted. He needed to pick up a few sniper rifles from the warehouse. As much as he hated shooting his opponents from a distance, he needed to be smart about his attack.

Even if he used the amulet he couldn't be sure he could take a sniper shot to the head, and he wasn't eager to test the idea. The simple solution would be to counter-snipe their shooters and then lay waste to the rest of the gangsters.

He didn't care who the message had come from. It gave him the information he needed, so now he didn't have to waste more time scouting the enemy. He was tired of running and wanted to return to what he did best—practicing offense as the best defense. There was no simpler strategy than that.

By day's end, he was going to make sure there were no Harriken left in Los Angeles.

---

Alison emerged from her late shower in a robe, with her hair up in a towel. "You'd think a magic school wouldn't have problems with their plumbing."

Shay laughed. "Well, they probably don't want you kids to become dependent on magic for everything. Or maybe the water spirits are hard to control." She snickered, then sighed. "I should probably talk about getting some other place to stay. Maybe an empty room. Don't want to annoy your roommate *too* much."

The teen shook her head. "Aya told me she's enjoying practicing being more social anyway. I guess having me as her roommate is helping her come out of her shell. At least, that's what she said."

"Always good to help people improve."

*Wonder if I'm helping Brownstone improve at all? The guy still seems as clueless as ever when it comes to anything other than taking down bad guys.*

Shay's phone rang, and she pulled it out, surprised at the caller ID. She gave Alison an apologetic smile.

"It's okay," the girl told her. "I'm sure it's important."

The field archaeologist considered taking the call out of the room, but decided it was pointless to try and hide anything from a girl who could see into her soul and knew when she was lying. Alison didn't need any more stress than she had already, between getting used to her new school and worrying about Brownstone.

"Hey, Peyton," Shay said, rubbing her neck. "I was going to call you in a couple of days. I haven't forgotten. I'm still working on making sure everything's safe for you. Just got done with a job not all that long ago to earn a few favors to make that happen."

Something rare flashed through the field archaeologist: guilt.

"Don't worry about it," Peyton reassured her. "I'm supposed to be dead, remember? Just like you. So big deal if it takes me a little longer to come back to life. I've got my Mountain Dew and pizza. It's all good."

"Yeah, I know. It's just… I'm going to help you. I want you to know that. I've got some people working on setting up a new life for you, but it's been going slowly. I didn't want to push too hard and maybe alert someone back East who might be looking for either of us."

"I know you've got my back on this." Peyton sighed. "Seriously, Shay, don't beat yourself up. You didn't have to pull me out of the crap, and I'll be grateful until the day I die that I don't have to continue working for the garbage that I'd been working for."

"Maybe all this is just about me having a useful contact. Ever thought of that?"

"Bullshit. You don't put yourself at that kind of risk for a researcher who is good with computers, especially when you're changing into a career where those talents won't be as useful. I don't know why it bothers you so much to just admit you wanted to help me."

"Okay, okay." Shay sighed. "That said, and not to be a bitch—or at least more of one—but what are you calling about, then?"

"I keep my ear to the ground to keep in practice. Just because I'm supposedly dead doesn't mean I can't collect info."

"Yeah, and?"

"I spotted something I thought was interesting, and I just wanted to make sure you were aware of it because it has to do with your new best friend." Peyton chuckled suggestively.

*We're not fucking. Not even sure Brownstone's straight. And if he is, he absolutely redefines clueless.*

"Brownstone?" Shay frowned.

"Yeah."

"What about him?"

"Not him, exactly. It's just that an organizational dead-or-alive bounty just went out for the Harriken in LA."

Shay gasped. "Are you fucking *kidding* me?"

"Nope. Just thought you should know."

"I wonder if *he* knows."

"Probably," Peyton replied. "The dude is a bounty hunter."

"Thanks, Peyton. I'll be in touch." Shay pressed End and stared at the phone for a moment.

Alison cleared her throat, drawing Shay's attention. "What was that about James?"

"A friend of mine let me know there's effectively dead-or-alive bounties now on every Harriken in LA." Shay watched Alison for a moment, awaiting her reaction.

The teen's expression didn't change. "That means James is going to go kill them all, doesn't it?"

Shay let out a long sigh and nodded. "Yeah, that's what I'd expect. I don't quite understand what happened with the Marines and he hasn't sent me a message about it yet, but from what I can tell that means the only people he has to worry about are the Harriken."

The girl nodded. "Good."

Shay eyed her. "Good?"

"They are bad men, and they shouldn't have tried to hurt James, and they shouldn't have hurt my mom. Now they'll get what's coming to them." Her expression darkened, and she turned away.

Shay didn't respond, struck by how well the girl was taking the whole thing. It was like she was growing up right in front of her eyes. But at the same time, the idea that Alison might grow into a jaded woman like herself didn't sit too well with her.

Alison pulled the towel off her head and Shay bit down on the gasp that threatened to emerge. The girl had been in the shower when Shay'd returned from talking with the school staff, which meant the woman hadn't had a chance to look for any changes; not that she would have expected any.

The teen's hair had grown several inches overnight. Now, instead of a few white tips at the end of her black hair, she had inches of white hair.

Shay's stomach tightened. She didn't know enough about magic, Oricerans in general, or Drow in particular to begin to understand how the girl might be influenced by her mother's side.

After seeing the aftermath of the carnage Alison's mother had meted out to the Grayson mercenaries, even a hardened ex-killer like Shay couldn't help her being a bit worried. People's ability to deal death and destruction used to be limited by strength and technology, but Oriceran magic had changed everything.

Was something of her mother coming out in her, or was this just how the Drow were? Alison seemed much more bloodthirsty than Shay'd seen her in a while.

*No. She's at this school. They'll help her control shit, and it's not like she doesn't have a right to be pissed at the Harriken. She's...not me. And she won't turn into me. Brownstone and I will make sure of it.*

Shay stared at the girl, troubled.

## 21

The wind howled over the rooftop. Other than the wind, the weather was nice. No clouds. No rain. Not too hot. Not too cold. It was perfect weather to annihilate the Harriken.

James' phone buzzed, and he glanced down at the text message.

**Perimeter secure.**

He nodded to himself and laid down behind the sniper rifle he'd set up on the rooftop, which was a couple hundred yards from the Harriken's temporary headquarters. They had taken over a six-story building in the financial district.

Before he charged in, he needed to take out their snipers.

Thanks to the anonymous message he'd received, he knew the most likely positions of the enemy snipers, or at least he believed he did. Now it was time to find out if someone was trying to set him up.

James wasn't worried that the snipers wouldn't be ready and waiting to shoot him. He knew they'd already be set up, especially since he'd made a point of calling the Harriken building to tell them he was coming—though mostly he'd wanted his enemy to be afraid. More than that, he *needed* them to be afraid.

The Harriken had destroyed his simple life, and he was going to show them why that had been the worst mistake their group had ever made.

James glanced through the scope, moving the rifle from target to target. Four snipers, right where his mystery informant had indicated. The Harriken valued face-to-face combat almost as much as he did, which would make clearing out their few long-range defenses easy.

He lined up the shot on the first sniper, who was pacing near a window on the fourth floor. The rifle cracked, and James didn't even wait to see the man go down before he lined up the next shot and jacked another round into the chamber.

The next sniper rushed to the window just in time to take a .50-caliber round in the head. Whether from hearing the shots or a radio transmission, the third man seemed to realize what was going on. He had already turned to run when James took him out.

At least they were going down quickly.

James lined up his final shot only to find the other sniper ready for him, rifle resting on the rail of a balcony and aiming his way. The Harriken sniper adjusted his aim slightly.

*Shit. He's got a bead on me.*

James squeezed off a shot, and the enemy sniper fired

half a second later. Deadly lead whizzed by a mere inch from James' face, the warmth of the bullet making the hair on his neck stand up. It hit the roof of the building with a loud plink, sending up a spark.

Fucking hell, that had been too close.

*See, Trey? Sometimes it's just about getting lucky. Of course, I'm sure Nana would have just marched in there and deflected their rounds with her cane like some sort of Jedi.*

James rolled to the side and peered through the scope. The enemy sniper was slumped over the rail, head hanging and blood dripping down to the street below.

The bounty hunter hopped to his feet and snatched his preloaded tactical harness. He slipped it on and took a moment to verify his loadout: weapons, ammunition, grenades, knives, and potions.

"Just like Shay hates," James mused as he pulled his torn and shabby gray coat from the rooftop next to him and grinned. It wasn't like he needed to hide his weapons this time, but he was beginning to wonder if this kind of coat might be a good luck charm for him.

He lifted the rifle from its mount and slipped it into its bag. The mount followed, and then he zipped the bag closed. The police would recover the weapon later if he couldn't.

Time to do this shit.

James threw the door open to the stairwell and stepped inside, then reached under his shirt and yanked away the piece of metal separating the amulet from his chest. The bounty hunter gritted his teeth; pain spread from the contact point and swept over his body as the amulet sank into his chest, and soon an inferno of pain engulfed his entire body.

He took a few deep cleansing breaths as the pain began to ebb. The now familiar if still unintelligible whispers rose in his mind.

The bonding process was complete once again.

James made his way down the four flights of stairs and then out through the lobby to the street. Police vehicles and police officers had created a perimeter around the Harriken building and a dozen drones patrolled the skies.

He made his way toward a now-familiar detective in a Kevlar vest: Delroy Washington.

"Detective." James nodded politely.

The Gang Task Force detective nodded back. "We already took out their security drones, so you just have to clean out the inside." He gestured to a nearby line of cops. "Just to be clear, Brownstone, no one's here to save your ass. We're here to make sure no one stumbles into this and gets caught in the crossfire. If this shit goes south a lot of cops—including me—are going to look like dumbasses, and it's not going to make us happy with you."

James grunted. "I was gonna do this with or without your help, so don't worry about it." His gaze flicked over to two AET vans parked farther back. Black-armored AET team members stood in front of the vans, weapons at the ready. Most wore helmets, but a brown-haired woman who was still holding her helmet glared at him.

The bounty hunter nodded toward the woman. "This isn't gonna be one of those times where the cops arrest my ass at the end, right? That AET chick over there seems like she's aching to take me down."

"Lieutenant Hall doesn't trust you, and yeah, she pretty much *is* aching to take you down." Detective Washington shrugged. "But if you limit the violence and destruction to the Harriken, she's only going to be able to make sure you have to pay some fines for your antics the last few days."

"'Antics?' You mean trying not to get killed?"

The detective chuckled. "Whatever you want to call it, Brownstone."

James sighed and rubbed the back of the neck. "I guess I better earn a lot of bounty money taking out these Harriken, then."

"You better. You should see the list of fines we already have for your ass."

"Is it a—"

"We've got movement," yelled a uniformed officer.

The police reacted as one, readying weapons and setting up behind their vehicles. Lieutenant Hall slapped on her helmet and the red goggles started glowing a few seconds later. She picked up an assault rifle with a grenade launcher attached.

James yanked a .45 from a shoulder holster.

*Frontal assault? Who do you guys think you are? Me?*

About ten people ran out of the building and the police all leveled their weapons at them.

"This is the LAPD," announced a voice from a large drone's speaker. "Advance with your hands up. Do not make any sudden movements."

The people all put their hands up, but they didn't slow down. As they got closer it became clear they weren't a threat, and most of the police lowered their weapons.

These weren't Harriken enforcers with guns and

swords charging the police in a brave frontal assault, but rather scared women, some in kimonos and some in business attire.

"We knew there might be non-combatants inside," Washington told him, "but we didn't have intel on how many."

James nodded. "At least the Harriken have a small slice of honor."

The detective looked at James. "That going to stop you from killing them all?"

The bounty hunter shrugged. "You guys were the ones who pushed a dead-or-alive bounty."

"Just asking."

"Nope. They die. Showing a little honor at the end is bullshit when they were willing to kidnap a little girl and *did* murder my dog."

He watched as the women made it to the police line and the officers ushered them to safety behind the police cars.

James waited about thirty more seconds, and when there was no more movement he stepped forward.

"Brownstone," Detective Washington called. "Good luck."

"Thanks. Is the surprise ready?"

"Yeah."

"Wait until I'm almost to the doors, then do it."

*You let the innocent people go. Good. That tells me you understand you're gonna die. Good.*

*You should have just left me the fuck alone.*

Jiro glared at the phone in his hand, wishing his conversation partner was in the room with him so he could shove his sword through the cowardly and dishonorable son-of-a-whore's stomach.

"I'm sorry, Mr. Ikeda," the senator replied. "There's nothing I can do. I took steps in the past to ensure this sort of thing wasn't applied to you, but it's out of my hands this time."

"*Nothing you can do?* You have allowed a dishonorable bounty to be placed on my people. We do not pay you for such annoyances to occur. You would not have been re-elected without our financial support—and our taking care of the witnesses to some of your indiscretions."

The senator cleared his throat. "This isn't my fault, and it's not like I have control of everything in the state. You were supposed to keep this shit under control. If you hadn't tried to turn Southern California into a damned war zone none of this ever would have happened. You couldn't be satisfied with drugs, smuggling, and prostitution?"

"You will show me respect me, Senator," Jiro hissed. He took a deep breath. "Your very poor quality of service forces me to modify our agreement. We will need to seek someone else—someone who keeps his word—and we will consider disposing of those who don't."

The senator laughed. "You're threatening me now, Ikeda? You won't be around tomorrow to worry about me, but if by some miracle you do survive, call me. I'm sure we can work something out. Good luck."

Jiro slammed the phone down so hard the receiver cracked. The senator would die as soon Brownstone was dealt with, and the Harriken leader would make sure the man suffered greatly first.

Such disrespect would not be tolerated.

Jiro stared down at the bandaged stump where his left hand used to be. He couldn't fail. Death awaited him, and with torture beforehand for repeated failure. The death of a single man would redeem his honor.

His gaze flicked to the monitor on his desk, which was displaying security camera feeds. He spotted Brownstone walking with slow deliberation toward the plaza in front of the building.

"You are brave, Brownstone," Jiro murmured. "No one will deny that, but that doesn't change the fact that I must kill you."

Jiro took several deep breaths, his heart thundering and his palm sweaty. His men had their orders, and he'd brought in reinforcements from all over the country. This was where the Harriken would make their stand in the United States. This was where they would prove why they were powerful.

The slain Harriken in Los Angeles had taken Brownstone lightly and paid for it, but those here would make *him* pay for every inch of this building. Engaging the man outside where police snipers or drones might help him was foolish, but it wasn't hard to notice the police seemed reluctant to join Brownstone in his direct invasion.

*He's only one man, and he will die. Then what? Will you come and arrest us? Would you dare after we kill your champion?*

The Harriken leader pressed a button on his desk.

"Yes, Mr. Ikeda?" a man responded over the intercom.

"Make sure the special teams have the necessary artifacts. Today James Brownstone dies and we reclaim the honor of the Harriken."

"Yes, Mr. Ikeda!"

Jiro watched, his eyes narrowed, as Brownstone closed on the building. The lights and computer suddenly died, and a few seconds later dim emergency lighting kicked in, painting the room in eerie red light.

"We will not run, Brownstone," the Harriken leader muttered. "And I will personally deliver your head to Grandfather."

## 22

James fired several rounds to shatter the glass of the front door and threw a grenade inside. He spotted the red-tinged outlines of several Harriken diving to the side.

*Might as well go all out.*

His left hand shot up and he concentrated on the grenade, which was halted by his telekinesis. He pushed it toward the escaping men and their screams filled the lobby as it exploded.

James tossed another grenade and pushed to the other side. He charged into the lobby after the second explosion.

Dead and dying Harriken filled the room. A moving shadow caught his attention and he blasted it with his .45, nailing a man who had popped up from behind the scorched reception desk. He took several small steps forward, then rushed around the desk. Only the single dead Harriken lay there.

James stared up at a security camera in the corner of

the lobby for several seconds, then waved and shot out the camera. He didn't care if they knew where he was; he mostly just wanted them to sweat a little.

*Hi, assholes.*

He proceeded down the hallway, ignoring the elevator for safety reasons. Even with the amulet, it'd be far too easy to ambush him with explosives or destroy the elevator.

Nope, there was no way around it. It was another leg day in the gym of life.

He would hit the stairs once he had secured this level. Although he assumed most of the enemy would come at him as he got closer to their boss, it wouldn't be smart to start out by allowing the Harriken to easily flank him.

The bounty hunter moved down the hallway, kicking in doors and sweeping the empty office suites. The slap of a magazine being slammed into a weapon echoed down the hallway, and he spotted a large sign.

"Cafeteria, huh?"

James crept down the darkened hallway holding his gun with both hands. He had a single grenade left, but he wanted to save it for someone who might need a little extra pain. He slowed as he approached the end of the hall. It opened into a wide cafeteria filled with round white tables.

A couple of red beams swept across the room before dropping.

*Fancy sights too, huh?*

He took a deep breath, raised his weapon, and charged into the room. Red beams converged on him, and a dozen Harriken popped up on either side of the room. The room erupted in gunfire and James leaped forward, sending round after round to one side of the room. Harriken dropped with cries of pain.

From the start of the battle, the amulet had whispered in his mind in its strange unintelligible language. Even if he didn't understand the words, each kill seemed to excite whatever strange consciousness was responsible for the whispers.

*Liking your sacrifices?*

Bullet after bullet struck him, sending jolts of pain through his body but not penetrating his hardened skin. James rolled behind a table and kicked it over to form a makeshift shield. More bullets pierced the plastic table.

He loaded a new magazine and finished off the Harriken on one side of the room, with six more on the other side in need of lead therapy.

He popped up and nailed one of the men with his .45. Two others fired, and one bullet hit him. He grunted and dropped. Without the power of the amulet he would have already been dead, but he also wouldn't have charged into the room.

The Harriken whispered something amongst themselves in Japanese.

*Really got to learn Japanese if I'm gonna be fighting Japanese gangs. After today though, I hope none of them are stupid enough to go after me again.*

He thought for a moment as he listened to the men. *Shay better not drag my ass to Japan anytime soon.*

The enemy started firing over James' head. He wasn't certain why they had done so until he saw the outline of the grenade coming at him.

"Shit." James dove the opposite way, not eager to test

whether his amulet would let him survive taking a grenade at point-blank range.

The grenade exploded a second later, knocking James against a wall. He slid down and clutched his stomach. Several bits of shrapnel had pierced his increasingly shabby coat, but he had only minor scratches and burns from the blast.

*Not quite, fuckers.*

His attackers, overconfident at their apparent win, charged from the other side of the room. Without standing, James aimed at them and emptied his magazine into the charging men.

He then pushed off the ground and reloaded. He suspected he'd have to borrow a few Harriken guns before the end of the assault, so he checked their weapons.

"Why can't you guys use my preferred guns? It'd be way more convenient for me," he muttered.

James confirmed that the men were all dead or dying. He wasn't going to waste a bullet finishing off anyone who was already bleeding out.

Not a lot of guys on the first level, and this probably wasn't their main force. Where were they, around the boss?

He let out a long sigh. It was time to hit the second floor.

---

James took the stairs two at a time, surprised when no Harriken showered bullets on him. He waited at the heavy metal door to the second floor for a moment before giving it a slight yank.

The darkened room lit up with muzzle flashes and the force of dozens of bullets hitting the door slammed it backward. James flattened himself against the wall of the stairwell as the men continued firing. The amulet strengthened him but didn't make him invulnerable as far as he knew, and he had a whole building of men still left to kill.

The gunfire stopped, and James flipped around the corner, shooting. Three men dropped, but the remaining six returned fire with submachine guns. James kept running and slid through a doorway.

The room was mostly empty except for a few tables and chairs and his current hiding spot, which was made possible by a short wall, and a small alcove with a coffee machine, coffee packets, and creamer on a counter.

"Even gangsters need coffee breaks," James muttered.

Bullets ripped through the partition.

"If they keep sending these assholes at me in these small groups this won't even be any fu—"

A massive explosion flung James backward and he crashed into a wall and fell to the floor with a groan, aches all over his body. He shook his head.

What the fuck was *that?*

The footfalls of the advancing Harriken reclaimed his focus. The partition separating the alcove was mostly gone.

James snapped his gun up and took down five of the men. Most managed a single shot or bursts of return fire, but the bullets bounced off James' amulet-enhanced skin. He gritted his teeth at the pain, but none of the bullets caused a serious wound.

The bounty hunter swept the room with his gaze,

looking for the final man. A Harriken holding a crossbow jumped up behind a chair in a darkened corner.

James chuckled. "Are you fucking kidding me?"

The unusual weapon made James pause and he didn't fire immediately, which turned out to be a mistake. The other man launched a bolt and a ghostly blue glow surrounded it as it flew.

"Oh, for fuck's sake! Magic. *Of course.*"

The bounty hunter jerked his body to the side; the bolt missed him and embedded itself in the wall behind him.

A blue fireball bloomed from the wall a second later, sending him right toward the wide-eyed Harriken crossbowman. James put three rounds into his body before hitting the floor and rolling.

After a few deep breaths, he got to his feet and looked down at the dead man.

"A crossbow? Seriously? Even if it was a magical bow, I still have a fucking gun. Never bring a magical crossbow to a gunfight."

James stared down at the crossbow for a second and then at the door opposite the one he had entered and slowly grinned. He picked up the crossbow and then searched the pockets of the dead man, finding a couple more bolts. He loaded the crossbow, aimed it at the wall, and fired.

The bolt passed through the wall and exploded in another blue fireball, showering the area with wood, metal, and drywall remnants. There were several muffled screams from the other side. James discarded the crossbow in favor of his gun and strode toward the now-huge hole, which revealed a broad hallway.

Shouts from one side of the hole revealed where the remaining men were.

*You guys need to learn to keep your mouths shut.*

James spun toward the sounds when he reached the hall, pulling the trigger again and again. Each bullet struck a man. His gun finally clicked empty and he charged toward the surviving Harriken.

The panicked men fired, some shots landing and others missing, but it didn't matter. James reached the end of the hallway and sent one man into the wall with a punch and snapped the neck of the other, shoving his body to the ground.

Aches, burns, and a few lacerations covered his body, but they were nothing he couldn't ignore. James reloaded and looked up and down the hallway. "Anyone else want to come out and play?"

The double doors at the end of the hallway flew off their hinges and a single Harriken with a violet aura and glowing red eyes charged through. He didn't have a gun, and his signature wakizashi remained in its scabbard.

"Okay, that makes things easier."

The Harriken glared at James.

"What's your deal, asshole?" James asked. "Do you go by 'Violet Glow,' 'the Master of Death,' or some other stupid shit?"

"I am Akira Nakamura," the man shouted. "And I have been honored by our leader with the power to kill you, *oni*."

Despite the fact the man was literally glowing James couldn't spot any obvious artifact, so he decided to try to end the confrontation the easy way. He raised his gun.

James shrugged. "Glowing purple isn't all that intimidating."

"Your arrogance will be your downfall."

"Maybe." The bounty hunter put three rounds into Akira.

The man didn't even twitch, just laughed. "Do you have any last words before I send you to hell, Brownstone?"

The bounty hunter holstered his weapon. "Is this some shit where the guy who made the artifact only wanted to punch people?"

As Akira charged James his scream echoed down the hallway. James sighed and met the man in a headlong rush.

The Harriken slammed his shoulder into James, sending him flying halfway down the hall. James landed rolling, and pushed up, rubbing his chest. Whatever Akira was using let him hit damn hard; even harder than Dmitri.

Akira chuckled. "The mighty James Brownstone. You're nothing in the end. Shall I kill you slowly, or show you mercy and give you a quick death?"

"Fuck you, asshole." James threw a knife at the Harriken, but it bounced off him harmlessly and clattered to the ground.

"Weak." Akira swaggered toward the bounty hunter with a grin on his face. He was obviously convinced he would win.

"Don't get too cocky, asshole," James warned him. "I'm just warming up." He sniffed and rubbed his nose with his arm. "And I've survived even though a lot of people have tried to blow me up over the last few days, so excuse me if I'm not impressed."

"Do you deny your heart gallops in fear, *oni?*"

James shrugged. "Not fear. Mostly annoyance. Anger. Vengeance, maybe." He scratched his cheek with his pistol's barrel. "Guess that's not really an emotion."

Akira charged at James again and threw another punch, and James lifted his arm to block the blow. Pain spiked through his arm as he slammed his foot into the Harriken's stomach. Akira stumbled back, grimacing.

James couldn't help but be disappointed. Usually when he had kicked a man like that he'd ended up in a wall.

"Tell me one thing, Nakamura." James requested as he shook out his aching arm. "I've heard that your big boss is in town. I just wanted to make sure he is here. Killing pawns gets boring after a while."

"You will not live to see Mr. Ikeda."

"I'm guessing you won't either." James lunged at him.

Akira brought up his fists but James dropped and slid at the last moment, slamming his fist into the man's groin as he passed him. The Harriken cried out and dropped to his knees.

*Hope nobody tries that shit on me.*

James hopped to his feet, grabbed the other man's head, and slammed his knee into it. Blood spurted from the man's nose. Not giving the man any time to recover, he smashed his fist into the man's face, knocking him flat.

He rained blow after blow on Akira and the floor beneath the Harriken cracked and caved in, along with the man's face. The glow vanished.

James stood and wiped the Harriken's blood off on his coat.

His hand hovered over his potions pouch, but he resisted the urge to grab the healing potion. He couldn't be sure how many more artifacts the Harriken might have ready. A few cuts, bruises, and burns he could deal with, and as far as he could tell he wasn't bleeding out.

*Wonder if a healing potion would grow back my arm if it got cut off?* He shook his head. *Don't have time to worry about that shit right now.*

James searched Akira's body to find the source of his power, but nothing obvious presented itself. Then he noticed a faint glow under the man's shirt and ripped it open.

"Huh. That's different. Nice ink."

A huge tattoo decorated the man's chest: an eight-headed, eight-tailed serpent. The tattoo glowed faintly violet but was fading quickly.

"Well, even *I'm* not so brutal as to skin a man," James muttered, and stood.

The bounty hunter hurried back through the hole in the wall. He picked up the crossbow and broke it over his knee. The weapon was too unwieldy to carry around with him, and he didn't want to risk someone shooting him in the back with an exploding magical quarrel.

He jogged back into the hallway and down toward the doorway Akira had redecorated. A cubicle farm filled the huge room, but the lack of reinforcements in the last fight suggested the room was empty. He stepped inside.

When he heard a whir, James managed to throw himself to the floor as a minigun blew a nearby cubicle into pieces. Wood and plastic shards flew into the air.

*That's what I fucking get for assuming.*

James chuckled when he spotted the gunner's feet. He

ignored the bullet storm shredding the room, concentrated, and put two quick shots into the man's feet.

The gunner yelled as he fell and the minigun's fire ripped into the ceiling. James wondered if he was lucky enough for the man to have taken down any of his compatriots with friendly fire.

He pulled out his last grenade and tossed it toward the man. Charging a heavy machine gun, even with his amulet, seemed about as dumb as trying to attack a hundred Marines.

After the explosion, James took a deep breath and stood, dusting off his pants and coat.

"Now, *he* knew how to have a proper gunfight."

## 23

About thirty minutes later, James made it to the stairwell leading to the sixth floor. He was out of the ammunition he'd brought with him, and all but one of his throwing knives were gone. He'd lost count of how many men he'd taken out, but he was pretty sure he'd already surpassed the combined total killed in his first two assaults against the Harriken. If the group didn't just flee the United States after this, they'd need to hold a serious recruiting drive.

*Learned your lesson yet, assholes? I know you're slow learners, but come on! How fucking stupid can you be?*

The bounty hunter had snagged a 9mm from a downed Harriken, but he didn't like the weight or feel of the weapon compared to either his .45s or his own backup 9mms. Two more artifact-wielding assholes had left him with a couple of minor wounds.

He'd never look at folding fans the same way again…or laugh at them either.

One of the artifact users had ended up with a knife in his throat and the other with about ten bullets in his chest. Fair enough trade, in his mind.

The amulet's whispers had become less excited and more measured, as if it were satisfied with his bloody progress. He didn't give a damn if the cursed thing was happy he had killed so many people. These men weren't exactly innocents. He'd confess his sins to Father McCartney later.

Right now, vengeance was his only concern.

James stepped into the stairwell with his pistol at the ready. He felt mild satisfaction with his progress, but mostly he was tired and annoyed. He was supposed to have been taking it easy the last few days, not having to kill half of Los Angeles because some stubborn assholes couldn't take a hint.

A hiss and a roar from above ripped him out of his thoughts and he lifted his head to see a rocket flying toward him. He leaped back into the room he'd just left before the projectile exploded on the landing, but the resulting fireball scorched him and the blast knocked him to the floor.

He rolled several times to quench the fire burning his coat and sighed down at it. Between the burns, tears, bullet holes, sword slashes, and magical-fan beams it was more a rag than a coat at this point. He pulled it off and tossed it on the floor.

"Rest in peace, coat. I'll buy your sibling soon enough."

His pants remained intact, but his shirt had more holes than fabric at this point. Light burns and lacerations covered his skin, but after killing scores of men and taking on multiple magical artifacts and several explosions he was doing pretty well all things considered.

There were footsteps on the stairs leading up.

James whipped up his borrowed 9mm and emptied his clip into the three Harriken who rushed in to confirm his death, then reloaded the gun and dashed into the stairwell. He fired upward, but no more rockets or Harriken came toward him.

*You assholes should have tried that shit earlier. You might have gotten lucky.*

He bounded up the steps. He found a discarded rocket launcher on the sixth-floor landing in front of the door, but no rockets.

"And always pack a spare," he muttered.

James glanced at the door. He assumed the final batch of Harriken enforcers lay beyond. If they had saved the best artifacts for their last line of defense, things might get a little dodgy.

A chuckle came out of his mouth as an idea popped into his head. He picked up the rocket launcher and set it on his shoulder.

James kicked the door open, and on the other side were thirty Harriken with their guns trained on the door. The room appeared to be a small auditorium.

"How about a little taste of a rocket, assholes?" he yelled as he charged them.

The men scattered like a cat afraid of a bath—none of them perceptive enough to realize the weapon wasn't loaded—and James hurled the empty rocket launcher to one side. It hit one of the Harriken with a loud thud, caving in the poor bastard's skull.

James whipped out his knife with his left hand and blazed away with the pilfered pistol in his right. By the time the Harriken realized he'd fooled them and tried to rally he was already in the middle of the room shooting, stabbing, and kicking.

James soon ran out of bullets and tossed the gun away. His knife, hands, and feet would be enough.

Dying men's screams overlapped and echoed in the room. Only fifteen were left now, and a charge with his knife ended with three more dead.

James yanked a man up by his throat and tossed him toward some of his friends. Several tried to shoot him, and the bounty hunter charged after him to throw a fist into one man's face and stab another in the throat.

Bullets bounced off his armored skin, their pain registering but their fatal purpose denied. He had to give the last Harriken some respect. None cut and ran, even as he pummeled and sliced each in turn.

The whole exchange was over in about two minutes. Thirty dead men lay on a floor freshly painted with their blood.

"No fucking artifacts?" the bounty hunter muttered, slipping his knife back into its sheath. He didn't even bother to loot a gun from the new collection littering the floor. "That's a surprise."

The only other exit was a single door at the back of the room, so James marched toward it.

Nowhere left to hide.

James kicked the door in, mostly to be an asshole. A short hallway led to an ornate set of wooden doors decorated with detailed carvings of roses. He stomped toward them but didn't bust down the doors out of respect for the woodworking.

It wasn't like the Harriken built the building; they'd just bought it.

James threw open the carved doors to reveal a reception area with desk and nice leather couches but no Harriken. One more door on the other end of the room stood between him and the completion of his vengeance.

The door opened, and a Japanese man stepped out. He wore a suit like most other Harriken, though the fabric was nicer from what James could tell. The man was a good fifteen or twenty years older than the bounty hunter and had white streaks in his dark hair. His sword was sheathed at his waist.

After a few seconds James realized the man was missing his left hand.

"Why aren't you wearing fancy Japanese clothes?" James asked.

"I look to the future, not the past."

"But you are the boss?"

"I am Jiro Ikeda," the man assured him, his voice filled with contempt. "I lead the Harriken in America."

"Best I can tell, there aren't many Harriken *left* in America." He glanced over his shoulder for a fraction of a second before returning his gaze to the main asshole. "Sorry about that."

Ikeda narrowed his eyes. "Such disrespect. You've slaughtered so many of our men. You should be on your knees begging my forgiveness."

"Why the fuck should I give *you* any respect? You torture women and kidnap girls. You should give me *your* respect. I've killed all your men, which proves that I'm big shit, Stumpy. Not you." James gestured toward the man's left arm.

The Harriken leader slid his sword out of its scabbard. James was far from an expert on swords, but Ikeda's sword looked longer and more curved than the blades he'd seen most of the Harriken use.

The amulet, which had mostly been quiet, suddenly started whispering loudly again in James' mind. Even though he couldn't understand it, he couldn't help but think it sounded frantic.

The bounty hunter ignored the whispers to concentrate on the man in front of him. He snorted. "Can you even use that sword with only one hand, asshole?"

"Your insolence is amusing." Ikeda raised the sword, smiling. "Do you know anything about Japanese history, *oni*?"

"Not really, no. I don't care a lot about shit unless it involves barbeque. But you guys have some nice barbeque-type stuff. Maybe I should look into that more."

"Cease your prattle! So you don't know who Masamune was?"

James shrugged. "Some Harriken dick? Did I kill him the first time?"

The corners of Ikeda's mouth turned down in a fierce sneer. "He was the greatest swordsmith this world has ever known. This blade was one of his greatest achievements, but the metallurgy he used to craft his blades has been lost to time. None have been able to replicate it. You should be honored that you will die on the blade of a Masamune *tachi*."

"Sure, asshole. I'll keep that in mind, but before I kill you there's something you need to do."

Ikeda shook his head. "You dare make demands of me?"

James snorted. "Yeah, I do. You're the one who is about to die." He gestured to the door. "Don't you get it, asshole? Your men are dead. I killed them all: the guy with the magic crossbow, the guy with the magic tattoo, fanboy, and helmet jerk. All those guys with grenades, guns, rocket launchers, swords—they are all fucking *dead*. And if that army couldn't stop me, you think you're gonna stop me with some fucking antique sword? That's not brave, that's fucking delusional."

"Such confidence. Such arrogance." Ikeda nodded once. "But I'll reward your bravery by indulging your whim in the last moments of your life. What demand do you dare make of me, *oni*? Tell me so I can laugh at your idiocy before I send you to join your dog."

"See? That's it right there. You need to apologize. Your men killed my dog, and because of you my house got blown up."

Ikeda snorted. "Your mongrel should have been fed to starving sharks a piece at the time."

James' heart rate kicked up and his hands curled into fists. "What the fuck did you just say?" The amulet whispered even more frantically.

"Are you as hard of hearing as you are stupid?" The Harriken spat and waved the sword. "I will enjoy taking your head off. I only wish I had your dog's head as well. I would stuff them both and put them on a stand in my office."

James charged Ikeda, bringing his fist up. Ikeda thrust

his blade at him, but the bounty hunter ignored the blow. He was unconcerned about a sword, since he'd been taking bullets, explosions, and various blade thrusts all day.

Agony blossomed through his abdomen and James looked down. Ikeda's sword was embedded in his stomach and there was blood seeping from the wound.

"No fucking way," the bounty hunter murmured.

The whispers grew quiet in his head, and something about them almost seemed disappointed.

Ikeda nodded, a satisfied smile on his face. "As I said, *oni*. This blade was one of Masamune's greatest achievements. It is not a mere sword. It is a powerful weapon with which a warrior can kill even *oni* or *kami*." The Harriken yanked the weapon out of James's stomach.

James stumbled backward, his blood splattering the ground and his insides on fire.

## 24

Ikeda sneered. "I do not know what *mahou* you use to make yourself strong or if you are an *oni* from Oriceran, but this blade is beyond your power. It is almost a defilement to use it to kill someone like you."

James grunted and kept holding his bleeding stomach. "One question before I die, asshole," he managed to spit out through gritted teeth.

"Such stubbornness to the end. Ask me your question and I'll answer before ending your life more mercifully than I should."

The bounty hunter flung his last throwing knife at Ikeda with all his remaining strength. Ikeda's eyes widened and he tried to turn away, but the blade pierced his throat. His sword clattered to the ground and he fell to his knees, gurgling.

"Guess that answers my question," James muttered. "Sword doesn't protect you. Violet Glow Boy was more impressive." He groaned and backed up until he found a wall, just trying to stay upright and ignore the agony in his stomach. *"Fuck*, this hurts."

The amulet's whispering was placid again, almost as if it were content.

*I win and you're happy, huh? Don't care that I got gutted? Fuck you, too, but thanks for the help today.*

The bounty hunter fumbled the healing potion out of his pouch and swallowed the contents. The seconds ticked away as the pain faded and his flesh mended before his eyes.

James slid down the wall to the floor and rested until every wound and burn on his body disappeared. He gulped down an energy potion next, shaking when the burn hit.

The bounty hunter stood up again and walked over to Ikeda's body, using his foot to flip it over.

"That was for Leeroy, Nicole, my fucking house, and my fucking truck. And for that matter, my fucking *signed recipe books*, asshole."

James marched past the body into the man's office, which was spartan and tastefully decorated. Several scrolls with Japanese calligraphy hung on the walls and several small stands containing knickknacks stood on either side of the room.

Ikeda's tastes ran to the expensive. One stand contained three cracked porcelain cups that had been repaired with gold. Gemstone-encrusted figurines stood on another.

"Got to pay for my house and my truck and that Humvee, jackass." James looked around and spotted a small garbage can, which he emptied on the floor. He filled the liner with Ikeda's valuables.

He rifled through Ikeda's desk, but there was nothing more of worth. Instead, he discovered something surprising and macabre: a jar with a severed hand floating in yellowish fluid.

James peered at it. "Looks like a lefty. That your missing hand, Stumpy?" He wondered if the man'd had to remove it as part of some sort of ritual. He took the jar with him, unsure what he was going to do with it but unwilling to leave it behind.

The bounty hunter stepped back into the reception room and realized Ikeda was wearing a rather expensive watch. Even if no one cared about the watch itself, all the diamonds in the thing had to be worth something.

"Huh," James grunted, eyeing his plastic bag full of loot. "I know Shay wants her fancy restaurant, but maybe I'll give her an artifact too as a thank you for staying with Alison."

His magical encounters in the building had all ended in the destruction of the artifacts—except for the enchanted tattoo, and he wasn't about to flay a man.

The Masamune blade all but shouted to him, so he picked it up. "I'm sure she can sell this to someone non-shitty for a decent amount of cash."

James made his way toward the exit. "Guess it won't hurt to check if there are any nice watches or jewelry on my way back down."

---

James eyed the garbage bag of loot as he sat in his second rental Humvee. It was all over. He only hoped this would finally stop the bastards from coming after him. Despite what everyone thought, even *he* didn't enjoy dealing with this level of violence.

*This week has been the most complicated I've had to deal with in a long time. Plans, asking for favors, a bunch of different magic shit. Fuck, I let that amulet have free reign, and it seemed like it was liking that killing.*

*How the hell can I KISS when I'm dealing with this kind of shit?*

There was nothing he could do about it now. He'd removed the amulet and didn't feel any different. That was a good sign, or at least he hoped it was.

James sighed and pulled out his phone to text Shay.

**Everything's over. Got you a present. Gonna call Alison in a sec.**

*Good,* Shay texted back. **What present?**

**A sword.**

**Haha. Just what every girl wants. What's next, a crossbow?**

James chuckled. Maybe he shouldn't have broken the crossbow.

He dialed Alison and the girl answered the phone on the first ring. "I was worried about you, James."

"It's all over now, kid. I'm sorry for any worries you had."

"And you're okay? You're not like crippled or something now?"

James chuckled. "Nope, not last time I checked. I mean, I have to replace a lot of stuff like my house and my truck's still being fixed, but I'm as tough as I was before all of this. You handling all this okay?"

Alison let out a quiet sigh. "It's okay. I think being in an actual school and learning about the world has helped me understand its dangers a little better. Maybe I've been a little naïve about the evils of the world."

James grunted. He doubted that a girl who'd had to deal with her father selling her mother to gangsters to be tortured until she surrendered a wish should be called naïve about any evils.

"It's okay to worry about people," he assured her. "The important thing is, the Harriken won't be messing with me for a long time, if ever. Not even sure there are that many left in the country."

"Don't worry, James. If you ever fall, I'll be there to wish you back."

James held his phone out to stare at it, wondering if Alison somehow knew about the wish her mother had passed to him to give the girl when she was ready. He'd avoided telling her about it, but now he wasn't so sure that had been the right call.

Among his other worries, he didn't know what would happen to it if he were killed. Alison deserved to receive her mother's legacy. Even though he'd stopped the hitmen and defeated the Harriken, that didn't mean he would win the next time.

James had almost fucked up. If he hadn't had the healing potion with him, there was a good chance he might have bled out.

His fight with Sombra during his recent trip to Mexico had left him unsettled and cocky at the same time. He'd defeated the necromancer without even knowing how, but the fight with Ikeda had proved that even a man James could normally kill easily could take him out.

It was like he'd told Trey: sometimes it all came down to luck.

"James, are you still there?" Alison asked.

"I might have something to give you when I next visit," the bounty hunter sputtered.

Alison laughed. "I don't need anything else from you. You already gave me my awesome necklace."

His neck tensed. "What *about* the necklace? Have you had to use it? Was there some sort of trouble at the school they didn't tell me about?"

"No, no, no. I mean, I wear it, but it's not like I've been attacked or anything. I haven't used it. Maybe I should test it."

"It works. Don't worry about that."

"I swear I can see jealousy in the energy of every girl here except for a few of my friends. There's even this one guy whose energy lights up with desire whenever he sees me in it."

"What the fuc— Huh? Desire…you mean like lust?" James curled his free hand into a fist, imagining showing up in some punk's dorm with a loaded .45 and making a point about gentlemanly behavior.

Alison giggled. "I guess you could say he's lusting."

"Who is this kid? Huh? Tell me his name so I can deal with him. Me and him need to have a one-way conversation about respect."

"Oh, it's not like *that*, James. He desires *the necklace*. Even in a magic school, it's not like everyone's walking around decked out in magical artifacts. Plus, it's really pretty. He might just want it because of that. Don't worry. I never take the necklace off, so it's not like he could get it even if he wanted it."

James grunted. "Still don't trust that guy. Maybe he thinks it's a way to get to you. You might be able to see people's feelings and stuff, but you can't read their thoughts."

"You're worrying too much."

"Maybe you could point him out when I visit next weekend. Not saying I'm gonna do anything, just saying a little warning goes a long way."

Alison laughed. "James, I can't have you beating up every boy who looks at me."

"Maybe not *every* boy…"

Shay said something in the background, but James couldn't make it out.

"Hey," Alison passed on, "Shay wants to talk to you really quick."

"Okay, go ahead and put her on."

There was rustling and scratching on the line for a few seconds.

"Hey, Brownstone," Shay exclaimed. "Glad you're still alive."

"So am I."

"Uh, yeah, well…"

"Problem, Shay?"

The woman sighed. "I need to let you know something, just so I can be honest. I think it's important to tell you after everything that's happened."

James' stomach tightened. He wasn't sure he could take any bad news after feeling so satisfied about finishing off the Harriken...and he still didn't like the whole boy situation.

"What?"

"I placed a big bet that you would survive all this shit."

"Huh? Wait, you're saying you gambled on whether I lived?"

"Well, I bet that you *would* live, so I was obviously expecting you to. Thanks. You made me a lot of money."

James laughed and the tension left him. "Glad I could be of service. If you ever need me to *die* for a bet, just let me know."

"Okay, will do."

"Oh, and about your present?"

"What about it?"

"It's a Masamune *tachi*. Valuable?"

"*Shit*, yes. Is that the present you got me?"

"Yeah, pulled it off the Harriken leader. You might want to clean it. It's got my blood on it."

Shay snickered. "Yuck, Brownstone. Try not to bleed all over the next artifact you pick up for me."

"I'll try, and thanks again for going to Virginia. It made things a lot easier." He rubbed the back of his neck.

"You're welcome, and just because you're giving me the sword doesn't mean you get out of the restaurant."

"Sure, whatever. You can pick the place."

*Not looking forward to some fancy place, but I do owe the woman.*

"Oh, you're gonna pay, Brownstone. Don't think you

won't." Shay sighed. "Okay, well, I'm gonna say goodbye to Alison. I guess I'll be back in LA soon. Maybe hit a bar before I head home. Not enough booze on this campus since it's filled with magical teenagers. They should be teaching them to turn water into wine. Now that would be magic!"

"Aunt *Shay!*" Alison shouted in the background.

James laughed and waited for Alison to get back on the phone.

---

Tyler gestured at the television. The news channel was running a story about the assault on the Harriken building and the chief of police was giving a prepared statement detailing the reasoning behind their obtaining of an extreme dead-or-alive organizational warrant.

"Okay, people," the bartender called. "We have official police confirmation of what went down and you're all free to check for yourself, but my sources indicate the contract's been withdrawn so I'm declaring all betting closed."

Half the bar groaned.

"What the hell?" Ben exclaimed. "How could that fucker survive all that? And how the *fuck* does he have the Marines working for him?"

Tyler shrugged. "He's got the Devil's own luck. What can I say? All I know is that Brownstone is alive and a lot of other guys are now dead."

Ben shoved up from the table at which he'd practically

lived for the last couple of days. "Between all this shit and your side bet, you made tons of damned money."

"Like I said, hedging my happiness." Tyler grinned. "And I don't give a shit what they say. Money *can* buy happiness."

He didn't want to admit he'd made several other private bets about Brownstone surviving. A lot of people were convinced the bounty hunter would ultimately die at the hands of the Harriken, but after the Camp Pendleton incident the bartender had become convinced of the opposite.

"Fuck," Ben muttered. "Maybe I should have thrown some money down on red."

---

Shay sipped her margarita. The Charlottesville bar she'd selected was a nice low-key place. Light country played in the background, but the crowd seemed more upscale than cowboy.

The ambiance was secondary. A little booze after the last few stressful days was hitting the spot.

Her gaze roamed the room. Two men at a table in the center caught her attention and made the hairs on the back of her neck stand up, but she couldn't figure out why.

*What am I missing?*

The men, both sipping beers, chatted quietly. There was nothing unusual about them, but something about the way they carried themselves insinuated itself into the back of her mind and wouldn't go away.

One of the men pulled out his phone and gestured to it and the other man leaned over and nodded.

*Go with instincts, but a little confirmation never hurts.*

Shay picked up her glass and walked toward the table, swaying and stumbling as if she were drunk. The men didn't take any notice of her; they were intent on chatting about whatever was on the phone.

She closed on their table and fake-tripped, letting out a yelp but keeping her drink upright. No reason to waste a perfectly good margarita. One of the men's hands shot out and grabbed her arm to stabilize her.

*Good reflexes. Very good reflexes. Nice muscle tone. Not a good sign.*

"I'm so sorry," Shay chirped in a higher-pitched voice than normal. "I guess I just can't hold my liquor." She giggled. "I got all turned around."

*Kill me now if I have to keep this shit up for very long.*

"Maybe you should stick to sitting," the man holding her arm told her. His gaze roamed her body and she resisted the urge to tell him off. She needed information, not sex.

With the men distracted Shay took her chance and glanced at the phone—and maintained her self-control when she spotted a picture of Alison.

The man holding the phone saw her looking his way and slipped the phone back into his pocket.

Shay forced another fake giggle even though it hurt her soul. "I'm gonna head back to the bar. I didn't realize how smashed I already am. Sorry, guys." She gave them a little wave and swayed back to the bar.

She took several deep breaths to try to slow her heart rate. There was no reason for the men to have a picture of Alison unless they were trying to get to Brownstone somehow. The contract had been canceled, so they wouldn't gain anything by going after the girl.

The ex-killer pulled out her own phone and held it up like she was going to take a selfie, but she made sure to angle the phone so the two men would be in the shot. After snapping the picture she forwarded it to Peyton and sent him a quick text.

**Need to know if these guys are trouble ASAP.**

Shay returned to sipping her drink and only occasionally glanced around the bar to verify the men were still there. A few minutes passed before Peyton texted her back.

**Both those guys are with Grayson PMC Services.**

**Thanks, Peyton. That's helpful.**

Shay sighed. The coincidence of two Grayson mercenaries being in a bar close to the School for Necessary Magic with a picture of Alison was far too great to ignore. She was going to have work a little to earn her magical sword after all.

*Jeeze. Almost feel bad taking that* tachi *from Brownstone. Honestly, the guy must not realize how much that thing is worth.*

Shay ordered another margarita and a glass of water. One trick she'd learned long ago was that if someone saw alcohol in front of a person they assumed they were drinking it. She needed the men—if they were aware of her at all—to just think she was another pretty drunk. That would be critical to the next part of her plan.

About twenty minutes later the men got up to leave, and Shay rose and headed to the front while they were still standing over their table. She hurried out of the bar and peeked into a nearby alley. The security camera near the end might make things difficult for her.

Shay stayed out of the camera's view. She recognized the model; it transmitted its video wirelessly. She pulled a tiny signal jammer out of her pocket and activated it.

"Can never be *too* paranoid."

"We doing this tonight or tomorrow, John?" a male voice asked. She recognized it as one of the Grayson men's. She smiled to herself and turned toward the front of the bar.

"You got something better to do?" the other mercenary wondered.

Shay sauntered their way as they walked down the street, heading, she presumed, to one of the parked vehicles lining the road.

"Hey, guys," she called, fluttering her eyelashes and speaking in that higher pitch again. "I drank...a lot tonight." She ran a hand up her side. "I'm Stephanie. What are your names?"

"I'm John," one of the men offered.

"Kendrik," the other chimed in.

Shay leaned forward. A low-cut dress rather than a T-shirt and leather jacket might have been helpful right about then, but acting would have to make up for it.

"Look, John, Kendrik," she continued. "I'm so sorry about tripping. I could have spilled my drink on one of you handsome men." She nodded toward the alley. "Maybe...I could make it up to you." She licked her lips suggestively.

The two men exchanged glances, lust flooding their eyes.

"In the alley?" John asked.

Shay bobbed her head. "I like it in the alley. It's hotter that way."

Kendrik grinned. "No shit?"

"No shit."

He looked at John.

The other man shrugged. "We can do the other thing tomorrow. Not like the girl's going anywhere."

*You're damn right Alison's not going anywhere.*

Shay sashayed into the alley and the two grinning men hurried after her.

Once they'd stepped out of the view of the street, Shay reached into her back pocket and gestured for John and Kendrik to come closer.

Both men stepped forward, eagerness on their faces.

Shay pulled out a stiletto switchblade and pressed the button, and the blade extended with a click.

"What was that?" John asked.

Shay smiled. "Nothing. Just the thing that's gonna kill you." She slashed his throat in a lightning-fast strike.

John fell to the ground with blood spraying from his throat.

Kendrik blinked. "What the—"

Shay didn't let him finish the sentence. "Sorry, but not, boys."

After cleaning the blade and returning the knife to her pocket, Shay fished some gloves out of her jacket and retrieved the men's wallets and phones. She could have Peyton deep-dive the phones later for information.

She pulled their guns out of their shoulder holsters and tossed them on the ground. She removed their credit cards and cash and dumped those too, hoping the police would realize this wasn't a simple robbery and pass the message on, even if indirectly.

"Your bosses will leave my niece alone or Brownstone won't be the only one with a vendetta."

The woman pulled out a small case and removed one of her cards, tapping it few times before putting it back.

"No. They'll just have to wonder."

## 25

James leaned against the Humvee with his arms crossed and stared at the remains of his house. Now that the Harriken had been handled and the contract was over he could begin to move on with his life and try to recapture the simplicity that had defined it until recent events.

A police siren blasted right behind him and he spun toward the source of the noise. The siren went silent, and James glared at the police car that had snuck up behind him somehow.

Sergeant Mack stepped out of the car.

"I knew you were there, dickhead," James grumped. "I was just lost in thought."

Mack laughed. "Whatever, Brownstone." He jerked his head at the house. "What're you going to do? Since my main job is bounty processing, I know how much money you bring in. You could buy a nice house and not have to live in this shitty neighborhood."

"But I *like* this shitty neighborhood," James mumbled. He stared at the house for a moment before continuing, "And I'm gonna rebuild. I've already got contractors and architects working on plans."

"Building a house? That's going to take a while."

"Not really. Even with all those fines I made a lot of money on the Harriken bounties, and like you said, I'm not exactly poor. When you've got more money than God and can throw it at people, they work a lot faster. Big surprise."

Mack chuckled. "Unless they are Oricerans who can cast an 'instant house' spell, you'll still have to live somewhere else for a while."

James shrugged. "There's a motel nearby I can stay in."

"Bullshit. There's no way I'm letting the city's best bounty hunter crash in some shitty motel."

"You got a better solution?" James asked.

The cop nodded. "Yeah, I do. Me and the missus own a studio apartment near our house that we rent out sometimes. It was supposed to be part of some grand real estate empire, but for now it's just the apartment." He shook a finger. "Don't think this is some big favor, Brownstone. You'll be paying me rent, and I'll have someone to talk barbecue with. The missus gets tired of hearing me talk about it."

James grinned. "Okay, if you need me to help you, I guess I can do that."

Mack nodded at the bounty hunter. "I'll see you around, Brownstone. I guess I'll be seeing you around a lot."

The sergeant got back into his car and pulled away, and as soon as he turned the corner Trey's F-350 burst around the opposite corner and sped toward James. The gang leader screeched to a halt and hopped out of his truck.

"That was timely," James remarked.

Trey's face scrunched up in confusion. "Huh?"

"Oh, the cop leaves and you show up."

The gang leader laughed. "Oh. Motherfucker, I saw that 5-0 and I was *not* gonna be around him. I was just staying away, Big Man." He looked up and down the street. "I've been hearing word that you're not abandoning our fine hood."

James nodded. "Yep. Rebuilding. Right here."

"How long will it take?"

"About four months." The bounty hunter nodded toward the burned-out ruins. "Maybe faster, but only if the contractors can leave materials on the site."

Trey rubbed his chin. "Okay, I hear you, motherfucker. No bitch-ass thieves will be stealing from your new motherfucking house. It ain't gonna be a good thing if anything goes missing, and if it does I'll make sure it's replaced by something better."

James stared at the gang leader in confusion for a moment, then shrugged. "Okay. Thanks, Trey."

"Welcome back, Mr. Brownstone. Welcome back."

---

Colonel Grayson narrowed his eyes at Major Tallmadge. "What do you mean they're dead?"

The major shrugged. "Both men were found dead in an alley, throats slit, wallets and phones gone."

"You're telling me two of our men were killed in a

simple mugging?" The colonel snorted and leaned back in his chair. "I don't believe it."

"I don't believe it either, Colonel."

"What do you mean?"

"Guns, credit cards, and cash were all left on scene. If it had been a robbery they wouldn't have left all those valuables behind."

Colonel Grayson took a deep breath and rubbed his forehead. "And we have absolute confirmation that Brownstone was in Los Angeles at the time?"

"Unless he can be in two places at once, he wasn't responsible for those men. There's absolutely no indication that he was in Virginia either."

"This man killed dozens of men because of a fucking dog," the colonel spat. "Our men just got caught in the crossfire. If those two men revealed they were with Grayson and Brownstone believes we've targeted his loved one he will come after us and finish us off."

Major Tallmadge shook his head. "But we don't have any bounties on us. We're a legal PMC services company."

Colonel Grayson slammed his fist on the desk. "There were no fucking bounties on the Harriken when he attacked them the first time and our men *still* ended up dead."

The major blinked and his face reddened, but he didn't reply.

The colonel took several deep breaths, his pulse still pounding in his ears. "Recall all of our men who are looking into the Brownstone matter. Let everyone know that Grayson will have nothing to do with James Brownstone, Class-Six bounty hunter. We won't accept any work offers or contracts that involve attacking him or defending people from him."

"What about the Harriken offer? It's a lot of money."

The colonel scoffed. "The Harriken are nothing in this city anymore, and probably nothing in this country. Let the fucking Harriken deal with Brownstone themselves. They're the ones who started all this shit. For now, we're going to keep out of Brownstone's crosshairs."

---

"Stop looking at your damned truck," Shay snapped, her tone sharp as a razor.

James chuckled and tore his gaze away from his newly-refurbished F-350. It was sitting in the parking lot right outside the window.

He focused on Shay and gestured around the dimly-lit restaurant. "Is this fancy enough for you? Even if it is a steakhouse, it's in Beverly Hills."

The woman was more than satisfied with the restaurant. Even though James had suggested she pick she forced *him* to in the end…and he'd done well. Surprisingly well.

"Maestro's is fine," Shay assured him, a smile creeping onto her face. "The waiters don't have towels over their arms, but the tablecloths are white." She gestured toward James. "And look at you, all fancy in your business casual. I like the sports coat, button-up, and slacks look on you, Brownstone. You clean up well."

James shrugged and looked down at his outfit. "I only had the clothes I was wearing at the time of the attack, and even *those* got shot up pretty badly, so I had to get a lot of new stuff."

"If you ever want fashion advice, I'll be glad to offer it."

Shay couldn't tell him right then and there how freaking delicious he looked in that outfit. She'd given up on trying to pretend to herself that she wasn't into him, but she still wasn't sure how he saw her, or even what kind of woman—or man for that matter—the bounty hunter might like.

"There's something I want to show you," James told her, reaching into his jacket.

Shay groaned and her eyes flicked around before she leaned towards him slightly and whispered, "You can't pull a gun in here. This is a nice place, Brownstone. I don't care *what* fancy new gun you bought."

James pulled out a small tubular authenticator device and placed it in front of her on the table. "Not being cultured isn't the same thing as being stupid, Shay." He pressed his thumb to the end. "It's ready to key itself to your DNA."

Shay eyed the device. "And this unlocks...what, exactly?" She pressed her thumb against the end and a burning sensation signaled the removal of the top layer of her skin. The device beeped and she slipped it into an accessory she didn't normally carry: a black clutch.

"It's the key to all your payments," James explained, "courtesy of the Harriken, for you having to drop everything and fly to Virginia. I've got a few things in a safety deposit box for you. The Masamune and a couple other things. It turns out that some porcelain cups repaired with gold Ikeda had were artifacts. I was going to sell them, but I figured I owed you more than the sword."

"*Kintsugi.* That's what it's called. The repairing-cracks-with-precious-metals thing. Gold, silver, platinum; all were used."

"Yeah, well, these magical *kintsugi* cups filter poison and maybe do some other stuff; I don't know. The Professor wasn't sure when I asked him."

Shay sighed, thinking about the value of the Masamune *tachi* and the cups.

It was too much.

"I didn't go to Virginia for a payday," she murmured. "I…" She shook her head. She couldn't tell him that she'd done it for him. "I did it for Alison."

"Doesn't matter. I'm pretty sure the Harriken wanted you to have them."

Shay barked out a laugh, covering her mouth. *"What?"*

James shrugged. "Well, at least I'm pretty sure they won't mind. I didn't get a chance to ask them before I killed them."

The woman smiled. She realized this was as close as Brownstone could get to saying thank you from the bottom of his heart, so she had to accept.

Shay grinned. "I'm glad the Harriken were feeling so generous, then."

---

The rest of the meal flowed pleasantly enough, and if anyone else were watching they would have thought the two were on a date.

Shay accepted that the dinner wasn't anything romantic; at least not to Brownstone, no matter how much that thought pricked her heart.

"I have to go use the can," James rumbled.

"Cultured, indeed," Shay said.

The bounty hunter smirked and headed toward the men's room.

Shay reflected for a moment on the pleasant evening they were having. She wondered if she could convince James to go out for another fancy meal, or if it'd take protecting Alison against killers again to earn that prize.

She hadn't told him about the Grayson men. As stoic as the bounty hunter was, she could tell the Harriken bullshit had taken its toll on him. He needed some downtime where he didn't have to worry about anything other than getting his life back to normal.

Shay had probed around with Peyton's help and learned that the mercenaries had decided to stay the fuck clear of Brownstone. They'd obviously received her message. Problem solved. All it had taken was slitting two men's throats in cold blood.

Two blonde women in little black dresses emerged from the hallway leading to the restrooms.

"Did you see that guy?" one of the blondes purred. "Not so hot on the face, but the rest of him was yummy. I'd like to ride that mountain of man-meat."

Shay's face twitched and five different ways of killing the women popped into her head as they passed her.

*Huh. So this is what jealousy feels like.*

By the time James returned to the table Shay had made

it up to a sixty-fourth way of taking out the blondes, each more painful than the last.

"Something wrong?" the bounty hunter asked. "You have a funny look on your face."

Shay shook her head and forced a smile. "Just thinking happy thoughts, Brownstone."

# EPILOGUE

"Bring it to me," Grandfather thundered. "I need to see it for myself."

The junior Harriken kneeling in front of him jumped to his feet and scurried off.

The global head of the Harriken sat in his chair reflecting upon the failures in America; failures brought about because of one man's vendetta.

Their operations in America had been crippled, and he would have to appoint a new leader to control the area. He wasn't sure their operations would ever recover after the losses they had taken.

He rubbed the bridge of his nose. "And all over a fucking *dog*."

The other man rushed back in carrying a hinged box. He stepped toward Grandfather cautiously and offered him the box with both hands.

Grandfather accepted the box and opened it; inside was a severed left hand packed in dry ice.

"Ikeda, you manage to disappoint me even in death."

# KILL THE WILLING

Did you know that Shay had her own series? Book one, Kill The Willing is available now.

Available at Amazon

## AUTHOR NOTES - MICHAEL ANDERLE

### WRITTEN APRIL 30, 2018

James rubbed his jaw as he looked down at the guy wearing a black t-shirt and blue jeans. "You want me to say something for your *Author Notes?*"

"Right!" Michael responded. "I think that since these stories are about you, Shay, and Alison, it would be nice if you said a few things. You know, 'meet the fans?'"

The Author started sweating; he could feel it on the back of his neck. Writing about James' exploits and actually looking up at the man were two completely different experiences.

"I'm not sure. That doesn't sound simple," James told him doubtfully. "Don't get me wrong; I appreciate you telling the stories, although having the people come up and offer their barbeque recipes to me from the back of the books was a little weird. However, a couple of those recipes were damned good."

"It won't be a problem. Look here." The Author pulled

out his iPhone, put it up to his face so it became active, and started looking for the app. He glanced up a moment later and caught a look of distaste on Brownstone's face. "Oh, technology…right. Not your favorite thing."

"It breaks," he grumped.

"Yeah, but it's cool, too. See, I'm going to turn on the recorder using an app. I don't have to carry around a…a…" The Author noticed James' expression. "Right, you don't *like* technology, but you aren't ignorant about it."

James eyed him. "Well, that's true as well, but I was more annoyed that you would even try to pitch me on the use of technology. Which part of 'I'm not fond of it' don't you understand?"

"Frankly, all of it," Mike responded, sliding the phone into his t-shirt pocket. "It makes my life so much easier."

"Until the battery dies?" James asked.

"Well, yeah, but that's why I have chargers by my bed, at my desk…" Michael had started lifting fingers and raised the third one. "And in the car, and I carry a ten-thousand milliampere battery plus a charging case I bought at the uhh…A…uh… fuck. The convention for audio and video." Michael grimaced. "That fucker cost me $85.00 and probably isn't worth $15. I was scammed."

James raised an eyebrow. "So you paid $85.00 for a special case to hold your phone so it didn't die?"

Michael shrugged. "Well, yeah. They use power. You can't carry the capabilities of a super-computer in your pocket and not expect to pay a cost in energy." Michael scoffed.

James looked at him. "How about I don't pay at all?"

Now Brownstone was just being aggravating. "Fine, ok. Simple life, happy life," Michael grumbled. "So, what's your favorite color?"

"Why would I have a favorite color?" he asked, clearly confused. "I could answer black, for shirts and my truck. Maybe a deep red for hiding blood. The white that is coming out in Alison's hair. Maybe that color on…" James stopped himself.

"Maybe what?" Michael asked.

"Doesn't matter, and hell no." He shook his head, "Not allowing anything like what I was thinking in the back of the book. There's enough of it coming out already."

Michael blew out a breath. It was a lot easier getting the demon Pandora to do his *Author Notes* for donuts than getting Brownstone to talk.

"What are your thoughts about the various woods used for smoking?" Michael asked.

James shrugged. "Depends on what type of meat you're working with. However, just about any properly-seasoned wood will beat any green wood you have if you don't know how to use it. The effort to burn through the moisture can provide some problems with too much smoke and heat. You will see the professionals with their large pits that can handle the heat use it with no problem. However, for most I don't suggest it. Now, for general efforts newbies can probably use oak as a good base. It will give you a medium-to-strong flavor that is seldom if ever overpowering. If you want to add some sweet flavor, perhaps apple or pecan. Now, if you are going to smoke a heavier meat like a beef or a pork, you will want to go with a hardwood. If you are going to do a lighter meat, like chicken or fish, you want a lighter hardwood. Don't ever…"

He looked Michael in the eyes to make sure he was paying attention.

"And I mean *ever*, use a resinous wood like pine or cedar. You will kill the food, and you run a good chance of ruining your smoker."

"Ok." Michael reached up to his pocket to pull out his phone and hit the stop button. "That wasn't so bad, was it?"

James eyed Michael. "You recorded all of that?"

Michael nodded, confirming that he'd hit the right buttons and now had the recording saved. "Yup, just have to transcribe it and add it to the end of the book. I'll tell the fans that we appreciate their support and their reviews, and certainly telling their friends about you guys. From there they can check out the Facebook group for our company and like it."

"They do all that?"

"Well, certainly. Some do, some don't. It's ok either way."

"Huh." He looked down at The Author, making him squirm just a bit. "So, let me tell you the right way to season wood…"

*Michael looked around, hoping something would happen to save him.*

—

I'd like to thank James for allowing me to interview him for these *Author's Notes*. I have no idea if I'll *EVER* do that again.

If you enjoyed it, hit us up in the reviews or over on Facebook or wherever and let us know. I'm sure I can get James to talk barbeque anytime, *anywhere*.

Ad Aeternitatem,

Michael Anderle

OTHER REVELATION OF ORICERAN
UNIVERSE BOOKS

## The Leira Chronicles

### * Martha Carr and Michael Anderle *

Waking Magic (1) - Release of Magic (2) - Protection of Magic (3) - Rule of Magic (4) - Dealing in Magic (5) - Theft of Magic (6) - Enemies of Magic (7) - Guardians of Magic (8)

## The Unbelievable Mr. Brownstone

### * Michael Anderle *

Feared by Hell (01) - Rejected by Heaven (02) - Eye For An Eye (03)

## The Soul Stone Mage Series

### * Sarah Noffke and Martha Carr *

House of Enchanted (1) - The Dark Forest (2) - Mountain of Truth (3) - Land of Terran (4) - New Egypt (5) - Lancothy (6) - Virgo (7)

## The Kacy Chronicles

### * A.L. Knorr and Martha Carr *

Descendant (1) - Ascendant (2) - Combatant (3) - Transcendent (4)

## The Midwest Magic Chronicles

**\* Flint Maxwell and Martha Carr\***

The Midwest Witch (1) - The Midwest Wanderer (2) - The Midwest Whisperer (3) - The Midwest War (4)

**The Fairhaven Chronicles**

**\* with S.M. Boyce \***

Glow (1) - Shimmer (2) - Ember (3) - Nightfall (4)

BOOKS BY MICHAEL ANDERLE

For a complete list of books by Michael Anderle, please visit

**www.lmbpn.com/ma-books/**

All LMBPN Audiobooks are Available at Audible.com and iTunes. For a complete list of audiobooks visit:

**www.lmbpn.com/audible**

CONNECT WITH MICHAEL ANDERLE

**Michael Anderle Social**
　　**Website:**
　　**http://kurtherianbooks.com/**

**Email List:**
　　**http://kurtherianbooks.com/email-list/**

**Facebook Here:**
　　https://www.facebook.com/OriceranUniverse/
　　https://www.facebook.com/TheKurtherianGambitBooks/

Made in the USA
Lexington, KY
10 January 2019